TOBEY REFLECTS UPON
THE WAGES OF GOING STEADY:

. . . School seemed even duller than usual . . . And I missed Dick rather more than I had expected to. Or maybe it was just the fun of having two men interested in me that I missed. Now if the phone rang, and a male voice asked for me, it would be Brose. There wouldn't be any element of uncertainty involved. But it wasn't that I was any less fond of Brose than before—it was just—

"Everything takes place in so good-natured a home atmosphere and is seen through the eyes of so likeable, honest a girl, that one puts down the book with a sense of having spent some time with people it is good to know"

—New York *Herald Tribune*

CLASS
RING

Rosamond du Jardin

A BERKLEY HIGHLAND BOOK
published by
BERKLEY PUBLISHING CORPORATION

To my son, Vic

Printing History
Lippincott edition published January, 1951
2nd Printing, October, 1951
3rd Printing, February, 1952
4th Printing, December, 1952
5th Printing, September, 1953
6th Printing, February, 1954
7th Printing, March, 1954
8th Printing, June, 1955
9th Printing, April, 1956
10th Printing, January, 1958
11th Printing, January, 1959
12th Printing, December, 1960
13th Printing, April, 1962
14th Printing, April, 1963

BERKLEY HIGHLAND EDITION, JULY, 1963

TENTH PRINTING

SBN 425-01321-9

BERKLEY HIGHLAND BOOKS are published by
Berkley Publishing Corporation,
200 Madison Avenue
New York, N.Y. 10016

Berkley Highland Books ® TM 758,135

Printed in the United States of America

Contents

Chapter One

FAMILY DISCUSSION

I HAD been wearing Brose Gilman's class ring almost a week before my family so much as noticed it. If that isn't just the way with families! Perfectly trivial details, like whether a girl's lipstick is a few shades darker than usual, or whether her loafers are beginning to look a little mellow, or whether she has finally succeeded in getting all her fingernails long enough to suit her—well, such things your family is aware of right away, even if they aren't really anybody's business but your own. But I went around for five whole days, practically waving my hand in their faces and not one of them paid the slightest attention to a big important thing like the ring I was wearing.

And that state of affairs could have gone on for years, I suppose, if it hadn't been for a perfectly harmless little scuffle I got into with my sister Midge one evening after dinner. I was lying on the floor in front of the radio, wearing rolled-up blue jeans and a T-shirt as usual, my knees pointing at the ceiling, my eyes closed, as I listened enthralled to my favorite disk-jockey. I didn't see Midge sneak up, bent and determined to tune in some infantile program that packed a terrific wallop for the not-quite-ten-year-old mind. Something dealing with some cowboy and his horse, you can be sure, since Midge has gone overboard in a big way for horses lately. Honestly, I don't know where all these mad fads that infect the younger generation come from. But Midge and all her little cronies dream horses, collect horse models, read horse books and sit entranced through every Western movie that comes

7

along. Now she proceeded to reach out and twist the radio dial so quietly that the singer I was listening to suddenly began to neigh. Naturally I sat up and grabbed for the dial, too. And in the brief but bitter struggle that followed, my hand just happened to bump Midge's hand pretty hard and my sister let out a howl of pain that made Mom and Dad both look up in annoyance from their respective sections of the evening paper.

"What on earth—" my father began.

But Midge's outraged complaint drowned him out. "She stabbed me! I didn't do anything to her and Tobey stabbed me with one of her old long fingernails! I'm bleeding!"

Mom said, "Tobey, really! I told you yesterday to file them down."

"I did, Mom," I tried to explain with the superior dignity of one who is being wrongfully accused and maliciously slandered. "I filed them practically down to the quick, just the way you insisted." I glared at Midge. "She isn't bleeding a bit. It was just my ring that sort of scraped against her buckle."

Midge squeezed her hand hard, trying to bring out a tiny drop of blood, and failed. "Anyway, it hurt something awful," she moaned. "Her ring must have awful sharp—" she broke off, staring at my finger, then her eyes lifted to my face in blank astonishment. "Why, that's not your ring, Tobey. It's bigger!"

Both my parents were looking at me, too. Mom's pretty, usually agreeable face was quite severe. And Dad frowned across the top of the sports page, which he had partially lowered, the better to settle this outbreak of hostilities between the only two of his four daughters still left at home. Since Alicia's marriage last June to Adam Wentworth and Janet's departure months ago for California, where she is now happily settled with her engineer husband, Jimmy Clark, and their four-year-old son, you'd have expected comparative calm and quiet to prevail in the Heydon household. But somehow Midge and I, without intending to at all, seemed to keep things in almost as hectic a state of upheaval as ever. Sometimes even I wondered how we managed it.

Now my glance fell demurely to the ring on my finger. I could feel myself coloring and I said softly, smiling just a little, "Yes, I know."

"Look, Mom, Daddy!" Midge's voice was shrill with excitement, her mortal injury of a minute before quite forgotten. "Tobey's wearing somebody else's class ring. And I'll bet I know whose, too!"

I smiled sort of mistily from one to the other of my astonished parents, ignoring Midge. These might not be just the circumstances I'd have chosen, but the moment had come. I held my hand up for their inspection, feeling the big ring deliciously loose and wobbly on my finger. "It's Brose's," I told them. "I thought you'd never notice!"

Midge said, with just a little awe mixed into the spitefulness of her tone, "*I* knew it was his, soon's I saw it."

"But, Tobey," Mom's voice sounded sort of chokey, "you should have told us right away. How long have you had it?"

"And where," Dad demanded gruffly, "is the perfectly good class ring I bought for you—the one I paid seventeen dollars and ninety-five cents for, of all the outrageous prices?"

My father isn't really tight, as this remark might make him sound. It's just that his position as the only man in the house sort of makes him feel he has to take a stand once in a while in financial matters. Besides, I had a hunch he was barking in order to cover up his softer, deeper emotions, as men are prone to do.

"I've had it since last Saturday," I answered Mom's question first. "Brose gave it to me the day after the Heart Hop. And as for my ring," I proceeded to relieve Dad's mind on the subject, "it's perfectly safe on Brose's key chain."

"That," Mom's tone rebuked Dad, "is not the important aspect of the situation as I see it.

"Seventeen dollars and ninety-five cents is important to me," Dad stuck to his guns, "even if none of the women in this house do have the faintest idea of the value of money."

"Henry, how can you speak of money at such a time?" Mom demanded. "I should think you'd be just a little curious to know what an exchange of class rings signifies nowadays. I am."

"So am I," Dad admitted. And all the nice deep laugh wrinkles at the corners of his eyes smoothed out, his face was so grave as he turned his inquiring glance in my direction.

Midge sniffed. "It means they're cuh-razy about each other. Didn't you know? I saw them yesterday afternoon, walking right down Main Street, holding hands."

I opened my mouth, but Mom interposed before I could put my blight of a little sister properly in her place. "Midge," Mom said firmly, "this discussion is between Tobey and us. You stay out of it."

Midge flopped down cross-legged in front of the radio. Her sandy hair swung against her cheeks and her expression was disdainful. "I'd rather listen to the Lone Ranger, anyway," she said. "Love makes me sick at my stomach."

Revoltingly, she burped. Honestly, what can you do about kid sisters? I gave her a nasty look before turning my full attention back to my parents.

"Well?" Mom's tone was gentle, but persistent. "Just what does your wearing Brose's class ring mean, Tobey?"

How could I put it into words so that Mom and Dad would understand, I wondered? Behind me I could hear the thundering pound of hoof-beats as Midge turned the radio volume up a little. At least, I was glad her attention was otherwise engaged. I walked over to sit gingerly on the edge of a chair opposite my parents. "It—" I groped for words, twisting the ring around and around on my finger, "it just means—that we're good friends, that we like each other a lot—" my voice ran down.

"Well, that sounds all right," Dad said relievedly.

"It's—nothing more than that?" Mom's glance sort of probed into me. "Nothing so serious as an engagement?"

I shook my head. "Oh, no, Mom. Really it isn't."

"An engagement!" Dad exploded. "Why, that's ridiculous, Laura. Tobey's only seventeen."

"I know," Mom smiled faintly. "I just wanted to be sure Tobey realized she was pretty young, too."

"Young!" Dad said. "Why, she's a mere child. And Brose—well, he's man-size, but that doesn't mean either of them is grown up enough to consider being engaged. Why, they'd have to wait years before they were old enough to—"

"We're not engaged," I tried to soothe him.

"They're simply good friends," Mom informed Dad. "She told us that. There's no use getting all carried away about it."

"Who's getting carried away?" Dad demanded irately. "You're the one who brought up the subject of engagements. Just because they've exchanged class rings—"

"I wore a boy's class ring once," Mom said dreamily. Her eyes had a faraway sort of look, her mouth curved in a little smile.

"You did?" I asked in surprise. Somehow you never seem to think of your parents doing things like that. "Was it Dad's?"

Mom shook her head.

"Your mother," Dad said with dignity, "was nearly twenty when I met her. She never told me about any youthful romantic attachments in her past. And she certainly wasn't wearing any ring that was several sizes too big for her when she got acquainted with me."

"You wrap string around them," Mom said in a remembering sort of way, "or thread. Is that what you did, Tobey?"

"Adhesive tape," I told her. "It stays better."

"May I inquire whose class ring?" Dad asked coldly.

"Why—I told you," I began.

But Dad interrupted aggrievedly, his reproachful gaze fixed on my mother, "Not that class ring. The one you wore, Laura."

Mom smiled. "You don't know him, Henry. His family

11

moved away from Edgewood right after we finished high school. His name was Detwiler—Gordon Detwiler."

It was an odd sort of name. I hoped Dad wouldn't make the mistake of laughing at it. Dad has quite a sense of humor, although his wit is a little corny, as is so often the case with older people. But apparently he didn't feel like making any jokes right now. Or else he sensed, just as I did, that Mom wouldn't like his laughing or making fun of the name of a boy whose class ring she had once worn.

"Thank you, Laura," Dad said in a kind of hurt tone, "for sharing this confidence with us. Sometime I'll tell you both all about the charming and devastatingly attractive women I fancied myself in love with in my younger days."

"I was never in love with Gordon," Mom said gently. "Any more than Tobey's in love with Brose. We were just good friends, we liked each other and had fun together, just as Tobey and Brose do. As for a class ring—well, that just puts a sort of seal on the friendship. Isn't that the way it is, Tobey?"

"Oh, yes," I nodded. "That's exactly how it is."

Mothers can be so understanding sometimes. Fathers, too. Of course there are other times when even fair-minded parents like mine can be ever so obstinate and difficult. But this wasn't one of those unhappy occasions.

For Dad was saying, with only a small note of warning in his voice, "Well, I guess it's all right then. So long as you don't go getting any foolish ideas about going steady." His voice seemed to underline those last two words. He went on, "I think you and Brose are both entirely too young to start that."

I drew a sort of deep breath and didn't say anything. But this was one of those times when silence wasn't golden. Dad frowned.

Mom probed quietly, "You aren't going steady, are you, Tobey?"

I swallowed. "Well—" I hesitated, "we haven't actually put it into so many words—but—"

Dad said firmly, "You settle that point, Tobey, and be

sure Brose understands. I won't have any such nonsense."

I told him unhappily, "Going steady doesn't mean any thing nearly so serious as most parents think. Why, I know girls who've gone steady with five or six different boys."

"Not, I trust, simultaneously," Dad said, a twinkle in his eye. That's a sample of the humor he's always pulling.

"Of course not." I chose to ignore the twinkle. "They go steady with one boy for a few months and then they go steady with somebody else. All it means is that—well, while you have this sort of understanding with a boy, you don't go out with any other boys, even if they ask you. Only, of course, none of the other boys do ask you when they know you're going steady."

"It sounds involved," Dad said.

"And dull," Mom put in. "At your age, I should think it would be a lot more fun to play the field."

"It's just a sort of—of security," I tried to explain. "If you have an understanding with one boy, then you know you're all set for the school dances and Friday night movies and everything. You don't have to worry about— maybe—not getting asked to things."

Dad threw up his hands. "I'm getting sick of the very word 'security' lately," he muttered. "Guess even the kids are reaching a point where they're afraid to take a chance, to trust their own capabilities. The trouble with the country today—"

"Please, dear," Mom soothed. "We're talking about Tobey and Brose, not politics."

I smiled gratefully at her. My father gets so worked up over politics.

"Well, yes," Dad agreed, calming down a bit "But I just want to be sure Brose understands this class ring busi ness doesn't entitle him to a full claim on Tobey's time and attention."

"He understands, Dad," I said. "We both do."

Mom reached over and patted my hand. "Of course, you do, dear. You and Brose are both quite sensible." She told Dad then, "Don't worry, Henry. I'm sure we can

13

trust them to work this whole matter out for themselves, without a lot of talk and interference on our part."

"I suppose so," Dad said, grinning at me. "Tobey usually succeeds in getting out of predicaments without too much trouble."

I smiled, too, although I didn't think it was very nice of my father to talk as though Brose were a predicament. Still, when Mom and Dad went back to reading the paper, I sat regarding their bent heads fondly for a minute, before getting up to go to my room and start in on my homework. They are really very sweet, as parents go. And I suppose Midge is no worse, actually, than any other little sister. I even went so far as to give Midge's head a light pat of affection as I went past her on my way to the hall. But Midge was so breathlessly intent on the Lone Ranger's adventures, she didn't notice.

Chapter Two

THE UNEXPECTED HAPPENS

BROSE and I stopped in at Joe's Grill for a malted on our way home from school the next day. It's funny how hungry we always get by three-thirty—makes it practically impossible to get all the way home without something to eat. Besides, Joe's is the favorite hang-out of the high school crowd. Simply everyone goes there after school, even if they're so broke they can't a⁓ rd anything but an ice cream cone. The place is always full of noise and color and movement, bright sweaters and plaid skirts and blue jeans, the juke box blaring, the lovely aroma of hamburgers making you drool. Joe himself is sort of small and bald headed and long past his own youth. His last name ends in -opolis and nobody knows how to pronounce it. I don't suppose Joe scarcely remembers what it is. Because he is Joe to everyone and we all love him. And Joe seems to love all of us.

He understands us better than most grownups do. He realizes that our pretenses and the silly stunts we pull don't mean anything except that we just don't want people to forget we're around. But we know we don't have to waste a lot of time and effort trying to impress Joe. We can just be ourselves. Sometimes the din around the soda fountain gets so deafening he has to yell, "Hey, quiet!" But nobody resents the admonition, coming from Joe. We even lower our voices—for a little while.

Brose and I managed to capture a corner booth and Brose brought our malteds over from the fountain. Service is something you more or less take care of yourself at Joe's. Brose is tall and broad-shouldered enough to push his way quite ruthlessly through the crowd, although our drinks sloshed over a little. His brown hair is the kind that would curl if he gave it the slightest bit of encouragement, which he never does. He grinned at me as he set our malteds down with a flourish and slid into the seat opposite. Our knees bumped against each other chummily.

"Guess what," I said. "My folks noticed your ring last night."

"Yeah?" Brose's eyebrows went up inquiringly, wrinkling his forehead a little. "What'd they say?"

"Oh—lots of things. You know how families go on."

"And how," Brose said feelingly.

Being an only child, Brose is the victim of considerably more concentrated attention from his parents than I am. In a way, it's better to be one of four children, even four girls. That way your folks have to spread their attention a little thinner to go around. And nobody gets overwhelmed with it.

"No objection on their part?" Brose asked.

I shook my head. My hair tickled my neck a little as it brushed back and forth with the slight movement. "No serious objection. Oh, you know how parents talk—we're so young and we mustn't concentrate on each other too exclusively and all that."

We smiled into each other's eyes and Brose reached out to give my hand a hard squeeze under the table. My heart

15

thumped a little faster as I took a deep sip of my drink.

"Can't think of anybody I'd rather concentrate on," Brose confided. "Not at the moment anyway."

I felt that way, too. Only, of course, I didn't come right out and say so. It never pays to let a boy think you're too fond of him, even when you're wearing his class ring. Things like that seem to go to the male head with disastrous results.

I said, "There's one thing I'm supposed to make clear to you. My father especially insisted on it."

Brose cracked, "He needn't worry. My intentions are honorable. I just haven't got around to asking for your hand yet."

"You'd better not," I told him drily, "or it'll mean the end of a beautiful friendship. That's what my father wants you to understand. We're *not* going steady."

"We're not?" Brose asked, frowning. "How come?"

"Well—you know we never said we were, not in so many words. That's what I told my parents."

"Yeah," Brose's tone was belligerent, "but when a girl wears a fella's class ring, it certainly means something!"

"Of course it does," I tried to soothe him.

"If it doesn't mean we've got a—well, a sort of an understanding, then I've been gypped!" Brose's chin stuck out with such fierce determination, I felt all quivery inside.

"Don't get all excited," I told him. "Of course we have an understanding."

"Yeah, but what does it amount to," Brose demanded, "if you're going to figure it's okay to go chasing out with every guy who asks you? What kind of a deal is that?"

"Who," I smiled my most inscrutable smile, "is going to ask me, when I'm wearing your class ring? You know how it is at school."

Brose thought about it for a minute, then he grinned. "That's right. All the fellas know you're my woman or you wouldn't swap rings with me."

"Exactly," I said, looking up at him beguilingly beneath my lashes as I sipped my drink.

"So, knowing I've got a prior claim, they keep strictly hands off," Brose went on, his grin widening.

"Right," I agreed. "But I didn't see any need to go into all of that with my parents. I mean, what would be the point of making a thing of it?"

"Sometimes," Brose told me admiringly, "you're so smart it scares me. And then again—"

"Okay," I said. "Let's drop the subject before you get insulting, shall we?"

Before long we were joined by Barbie Walters and Sox Trevor. Barbie is small and dark-haired and wears harlequin glasses and has been my closest friend since we were in grade school. And Sox is tall and thin and blond, with a bristling short haircut. They have been a regular twosome for quite a while now, so that everyone has got used to the difference in their height and has stopped making jokes about it. Sox set their sodas on the table and Brose and I squeezed over willingly to make room for them. Sox and Brose immediately embarked on a heated discussion of the chances of Edgewood High in the football game next Saturday. Barbie and I joined in and before it seemed possible to any of us it was four-thirty and time to get started for home. That's the way time always flies past at Joe's.

Outside, Main Street had assumed its regular late afternoon air of bustle and hurry. Edgewood is a sort of typical medium-sized town, with a business section covering a radius of several blocks and tree-lined residential streets crisscrossing off in all directions.

The four of us walked along together as far as we could, talking and laughing, scuffling the drifted brown and yellow leaves that covered the sidewalk. The late October sunshine felt warm across our shoulders, the blue sky was full of whipped-cream clouds. I love this time of year. It's fun in itself and ahead are all the good times of winter, skating and tobogganing, all the holidays.

"Before you know it," I said aloud, following my own train of thought, "it'll be Christmas."

The others hooted raucously.

"It's even weeks till Thanksgiving," Barbie said. "You're getting 'way ahead of yourself."

"That's right," I had to admit, laughing a little at myself. "I nearly forgot about Thanksgiving."

"She's nuts," Brose confided to the others, "but harmless—I think."

I made a face at him. "Could be the company I keep that's affecting me."

Barbie and Sox turned off at the next corner, calling, "So long" and "See you tomorrow." We strolled on till we came to the walk leading up to my house. It's a big, old-fashioned sort of place, but comfortable. Plenty of room and lots of porches and a big yard full of bushes and shade trees. Brose handed over my books and gave my shoulder a little pat.

"Gotta get going," he said. "I'm supposed to rake leaves before dinner."

"Okay," I smiled up at him. "Thanks for the malted."

"Any time," Brose said. And loped off, whistling.

I made my way up the front steps. On the porch Midge was crouched with her special friend, Judy Allen. Both of them looked grimy and disreputable as usual, their T-shirts hanging out over the tops of their shorts. Judy's shaggy dark head was very close to Midge's. All around them were their horse models, surrounded by the fences they made out of blocks and pieces of board. They had doll dishes, some filled with grass and some with water, set out for the horses to feed and drink from. Neither of them heard me coming, so intent were they on their game, till I said, "Hi, kids."

"Oh, hi," Midge said, without bothering to look up.

Judy wasted one glance on me. "Did you know one of Midge's horses just had a new colt?" she inquired seriously.

"No!" I pretended astonishment. "Which horse, Midge?"

"Metro Golden Mare," Midge said and, as always, her name for the gilt-colored horse model amused me. "And here's her colt, see?" She held up a white china colt with gilded hoofs my father had brought back for her from a recent business trip to Chicago.

"Very interesting," I said and went on into the house, smothering my laughter.

Still, I could remember how seriously I had taken my paper dolls and their affairs and problems not too many years back. Ah, imagination, I thought. What would kids do without it?

Mom's voice reached me from the kitchen along with a wonderful aroma of—could it be gingerbread? "Tobey, is that you?"

"Um-huh," I admitted, following my appreciative nose toward the back of the house. "Can I have a piece, Mom? I'm starved."

"It's not done yet," Mom said firmly. "And anyway, it's for dinner. You just save your appetite."

"I don't think I can last out," I said. "What else we having?"

"Meat loaf," Mom enumerated, "and baked potatoes and green beans and tossed salad. Meet with your approval?"

I nodded ecstatically. "All my favorite food."

"Good," Mom said drily. "Then you won't mind breaking up the beans for me."

"I've got homework." I held up my books. It was worth a try anyway.

"You can do it later," Mom said. "I'm a little swamped. I went to Woman's Club this afternoon and they had one of those speakers—oh, he was interesting enough, but he went on and on!"

She proceeded to tell me about the club meeting, while I fixed the beans. And I told her about a couple of funny things that had happened at school. Our kitchen is a sort of cozy place, people always seem to find it easy to talk and laugh a lot there. Getting the green beans on to cook was almost a painless process and went much faster than I had thought it would.

When the phone rang, Mom said, "You answer it.

Everything's under control around here now. I can finish up."

Could it be Brose, I wondered, lifting the phone from the hall table. "Hello?"

"Long distance calling," the operator said. Then a man's voice, tantalizingly familiar, inquired, "Is that you, Tobey?

"Yes." I frowned, leaning against the wall, kicking off my loafers in order to wiggle my toes more freely. I still hadn't the faintest idea who this was.

"Dick Allen," the deep amused voice at the other end of the wire said pleasantly. "Don't tell me you've forgotten me already.

"Oh—Dick!" My heart seemed to come up high in my throat and then flop back again. "Of course I haven't. I—just didn't recognize your voice for a minute."

How could I forget Judy Allen's good-looking brother? I had only met him once, but the circumstances of our one date had been such as to impress it indelibly on any girl's memory. A short while back, after a quarrel with Brose, I had found myself in the most ghastly predicament you can imagine. Humiliatingly, I was left high and dry without a date for the Heart Hop, one of the most important dances of the school year at Edgewood. Without the slightest co-operation on my part—I hadn't even known what the two wonderful little fiends were up to until the very night of the dance—Midge and Judy had pressed Dick into service as my escort. And Dick hadn't seemed to mind, he had appeared to enjoy the evening as much as I did—still, I'd hardly expected to hear from him so soon. After all, Dick was nineteen, a sophomore in college.

"You sound surprised," Dick's laugh was teasing.

"Wh—where are you?" I gulped.

"At school," he said. "All of seventy-five miles away. Quite a handy little gadget Mr. Bell invented."

"Yes, isn't it?" I agreed, easing up a little, not gripping the telephone quite so hard. "Expensive, though, for long-distance."

"What's money?" Dick scoffed. Then, mockingly aghast, "What am I saying? And me three jumps ahead of the finance company."

After a few minutes of such casual talk, Dick got to the point of the conversation. He asked, his voice thrillingly hopeful, "You're not all dated up for Thanksgiving week-end, are you, Tobey?"

"Thanksgiving?" I repeated faintly. "Why—that's weeks off."

"Only a little over three," Dick corrected. "And I wanted to ask you in plenty of time."

"Ask me—what?" Even I could detect the note of fearful fascination in my voice.

"Here's the pitch," Dick told me. "On Friday night we're having a small shindig at my fraternity house. Saturday's the big football game of the season—we're playing Dundee and it ought to be good. Then Saturday night there's the Inter-Fraternity dance, formal, big-name band, all the trimmings. I'd like to have you come up for all of it, Tobey. Think you can?"

"Oh—oh, Dick!" My heart was pounding, my eyes wide, my lips parted. A college dance—the kind I'd only heard about from my older sisters, that I hadn't expected to be invited to for ages! And Dick Allen, who was so sensational, such a smooth dancer, a date any girl would be proud of—he was asking me! Somehow, I couldn't believe it was actually happening, that I wasn't dreaming it. And then suddenly I remembered Brose—and knew I was wide awake. "Dick, I don't know—" my voice choked up.

I'd been going to say, "I don't know how to thank you. But I can't go—I'm sorry—" Only the words jammed up in my throat.

And Dick's easy voice reached me before I could go on. "Look, Tobey, I know how it is. You'll have to ask your folks and all. So how about if I call you tomorrow around this time? That'll give you a chance to work out the details and you can let me know for sure. So high-pressure 'em, girl. I'm counting on you. 'Bye."

" 'B-bye," my lips formed the single syllable dazedly.

And dazedly I hung up. The familiar atmosphere of the house closed in around me once more, bringing me back to the present. From the kitchen came the cheerful clatter of pans, the rich spicy odor of gingerbread. From the porch came the murmur of Midge's and Judy's voices as they went on tirelessly with their game of horses. Everything was the same—and yet different.

I sighed. A very deep sigh. For the first time since I had accepted it, Brose's ring seemed to weigh heavily on my finger.

Chapter Three

ACT OF FATE

IT WAS not until dinner time that Mom noticed there was something wrong with me. I had gone up to my room after talking with Dick and had stayed there, brooding and miserable, until I heard my father come in. I knew then it was just a matter of time till I got called downstairs to dinner, so I brushed my hair and freshened my lipstick and went down of my own accord. Midge was lying on the living-room floor on her stomach, reading the comics in the evening paper. Dad was out in the kitchen, talking to Mom. No one paid the slightest attention to me.

Finally we were all assembled around the dining table. Mom's meat-loaf is always delicious, but I could scarcely force a bite past my lips. The conversation swirled around me, but all I could think of was that formal inter-fraternity dance, the big-name band, Dick Allen's arm around me as we danced, his eyes smiling down into mine—only I wasn't going to be there! It would be some other girl dancing with Dick, smiling back at him, being a part of the whole wonderful scene. And where would I be? Probably going to a movie with Brose and, if his allowance held out, stopping at Joe's afterward for a malted

22

and a hamburger. I lifted a bite of salad to my mouth, then put it back on my plate untasted.

"Tobey," Mom's voice sounded anxious and, when I looked up at her, she was frowning, "don't you feel well?"

I nodded, not very convincingly, I guess. "I'm okay."

Mom's glance dropped to my plate. "But you're not eating. And you said before you were starved."

She looked up at me questioningly and Dad's eyes were fixed on my face, too. I gulped, "I was—but now I'm not—" I was afraid if I went on talking I'd burst into tears. But I couldn't. It would be too absurd. Still I couldn't seem to stop my lips from trembling.

"Baby, what is it? What's wrong?" Dad asked concernedly.

And Mom begged, "Tell us, dear."

So I told them. All about Dick's call and the small party at his fraternity house and the big game and the dance afterward. I finished, "And Dick wants me to be his guest for the whole week-end—and I could just die—"

My parents and Midge stared blankly at me, then Mom and Dad looked, with an equal lack of understanding, at each other. Midge was the first to speak. Her eyes were shining and her little freckled nose practically quivered with excitement.

"But, Tobey, that's super!" Having been an instigator of my first meeting with Dick, I suppose it was only natural for her to take a proprietary interest in any subsequent developments. "Why could you die, for creep's sake?"

Dad complained, "I don't get it, either."

And Mom asked, "Did you think we wouldn't let you go, Tobey?"

"Or is it because of a new dress?" Dad asked resignedly.

I swallowed. Why hadn't I just kept my mouth shut in the first place.

Mom said, "After all, for a big week-end like that, there must be ever so many girls invited. The college will have made suitable arrangements for putting them up. Or you could stay with Alicia and Adam if they have room. I don't see—"

Dad broke in, grinning a trifle wryly, "Don't let the fact that you haven't a thing to wear hold you back. I've been known to come through in a pinch before this."

It was Midge who came closest to the truth as she remarked, sniffing, "It's because of Brose, I'll bet. She wants to go with Dick, but she can't because Brose might not like it."

Dad frowned and Mom said, "But, surely, Tobey, you're free to have a date with any boy you care to."

"I told you just last night," Dad reminded severely, "this 'going steady' nonsense was out."

"I know," I said quickly. "It—isn't that exactly. I mean —there are lots of angles to a situation like this. I'm— fond of Brose. I wouldn't want to hurt his feelings."

"But you like Dick, too," Mom said. "You told me so yourself. And this sounds like such a very special occasion."

I nodded miserably. Did she think I didn't realize how special and wonderful it was? Her brown eyes that are so nearly the color of my own, were fixed intently on me. "Listen here, young lady," my father began sternly.

But Mom said reprovingly, "Now, Henry, remember Tobey isn't a child. She's capable of making her own decisions—" her voice grew wistful, "and yet—"

"I'll bet she's already turned him down," Midge said disdainfully. "Ill bet she just said 'no' right flat out."

"I did not!" I denied hotly. After all, there are limits to how much you can take from a little squirt her age. "And if I did, I can't see that it's any business of yours!"

"It is so," Midge argued. "If it hadn't been for Judy'n me, you might never have met Dick. And if you hadn't met him he couldn't have taken you to the Heart Hop. And if you ask me—"

"I didn't," I cut her off grimly. "And just remember that if it hadn't been for you, I'd have gone to the Heart Hop with Brose and wouldn't have needed Dick to take me. And anyway—"

"Girls," my father said warningly, "that's enough bickering. Honestly, you two can get into a fight faster—"

"Well, it's her fault!" Midge and I said, with such perfect timing that you'd have thought we'd rehearsed it. And then the way the words came out in a sort of duet struck us both a little funny and we started to laugh.

"At least," Dad said, "you haven't lost your sense of humor. That's a good thing."

"Tobey," Mom's tone was inquiring, "you say you didn't tell Dick you wouldn't go?"

I shook my head. "I didn't get a chance. He said he knew I'd have to ask you first, so he'd call me back tomorrow."

Mom said relievedly, "At least you'll have time then to think it over. You will do that, won't you, dear?"

"That's what I've been doing," I said miserably, "but it only makes me feel worse."

"But if you want to—" Dad began.

Mom stopped him with a little warning look. "Now, Henry, it's certainly up to Tobey to decide. Let's drop the subject for now, shall we?"

"Gladly!" Dad said on a slightly grim note.

Midge shook her head pityingly. "I just hope I don't get goofy when I get older."

The rest of the meal and the rest of the evening dragged past. I had quite a lot of homework—the teachers surely love to pile it on us Seniors, especially Miss Prescott in Math. But in between geometry problems I kept thinking of Dick and of how flattering it was for a girl to get asked to a big college dance. Why, he could have his pick of any number of girls his own age, students right there at Central University. But he preferred me and after having had only one date with me, too. I must have made a rather terrific impression. I sighed and turned on some dreamy music on my radio. But that didn't help any. It only made me feel worse, thinking of the big name band I was going to miss. I let my mind toy with the mad delicious idea of *not* missing it, of telling Dick I'd go. But then when Brose started lining up things for us to do Thanksgiving week-end and I had to tell him I wouldn't be available—no, I couldn't do that to Brose. I shivered a little, thinking how furious he'd be. Brose is inclined to be jealous anyway and the mere mention of Dick's name practically makes him emit sparks. It isn't that he has anything personal against Dick, he scarcely knows him. But Brose reacts that way to any boy he thinks I like pretty well. And I can't say I mind, really. But it certainly made the prospect of my spending a whole week-end in Dick's company at college utterly out of the question. Life is so difficult sometimes . . .

As usual I didn't see too much of Brose the next day at school. We only have a couple of classes together and our lunch hours don't coincide, so we hardly ever encounter each other except briefly sometimes in the hall between periods. But we always meet outside the east entrance after school and walk home together.

I must have looked a little glum when I joined Brose, because he asked, with his customary brutal candor, "What's eating you, keed? You get a pink slip, too?"

I shook my head. Pink slips are foul things the teachers at Edgewood hand out to you if your grades are falling a little below par, a sort of warning that you'd better buckle down to business if you want to get a passing grade on your next report card.

"What did you get one in?" I asked sympathetically.

"French," Brose groaned.

"Not again! But French is easy, Brose. Now geometry—"

"Any form of Math is a cinch," Brose said. "But French —well, you know how I struggle, Tobey. And you help me a lot. But—" he shrugged, "I should'a left it for the Frenchmen, I guess."

I tried to cheer him up as we headed for home. But even a stopover at Joe's for a soda didn't do much to snap him out of his despondency. He was so engrossed in his own troubles, he never did get back to trying to find out why I wasn't my usual bright gay self. And that I was grateful for.

When we reached my front walk, he asked, "Mind if I come in awhile? I thought maybe you'd give me a lift with my French assignment for tomorrow. It's a stinker."

My heart stopped. This was all I needed, Brose right at hand when Dick called up for his answer. I babbled, "I've got a million things to do now, Brose. Shampoo my hair and—oh, stuff like that. But if you come over after dinner, I'll be glad to help."

"Gee, will you, Tobey?" Brose said gratefully. "That'll be swell. And I'll sure appreciate it. Holy Sox, if I flunked a subject my last year, my folks'd have a fit."

"You won't," I assured him staunchly. "You've got lots of time. It won't even be the middle of the semester till Thanksgiving."

"Thanksgiving," Brose repeated darkly. "That's another headache. Boy, am I a guy with troubles."

"What do you mean?" I stared at him. I thought I was the one who was in a stew over Thanksgiving.

Brose sighed. "Gosh, Tobey, I was figuring, with a few days off from school, we could have a big time. And you know what my mother sprung on me last night?"

I shook my head.

"Right out of a clear sky she sprung it," he complained, kicking a stone off the sidewalk. "You know how my grandparents usually come to visit us Thanksgiving? Well, this year, due to my grandfather's not being so well, we're going there instead."

"Going—there?" I repeated not very intelligently. But my heart was starting to race and swoop in the craziest fashion.

"To Cleveland," Brose said disgustedly. "Almost four hundred miles. A trip like that'll shoot the whole week-end. But when I tried to talk my mother into letting me stay home, she wouldn't hear of it."

"Of—of course, your gradparents will want to see you, too," I said, keeping my tone gravely sympathetic, or at least as gravely sympathetic as I could in view of the way my spirits were lifting. Why, if Brose was going to be away the entire week-end, he could hardly expect me to simply spend the time twiddling my thumbs.

"That's what my mother says," Brose admitted. His unhappy glance came up to meet mine. "I couldn't talk her out of it—but honestly, I tried, Tobey."

"Sure, you did." I patted his hand forgivingly. "It's just one of those family entanglements everybody gets caught in now and then."

"And you won't hold it against me?" Brose asked.

"I should say not!" I assured him. "Why, something of the same sort might happen to me sometime, too. And I wouldn't want you to get mad at me over it."

"Gee, you're swell." Brose captured my hand in his big one and squeezed it hard. "You're so understanding, Tobey. That's what I like about you. Gosh, I was almost afraid to tell you, for fear you'd be sore. And here you aren't even making a thing of it."

I said faintly, feeling ashamed, "It's nothing to get sore over."

"What a woman!" Brose regarded me with profound admiration and I felt more ashamed than ever.

I gulped, "I have to go in now. Bring your French grammar and come over around seven-thirty."

"Will do," Brose grinned. "And thanks for everything."

He strode off and I went into the house slowly. By a sheer miraculous act of fate I was free now to accept Dick's thrilling invitation. Brose wouldn't even know about it unless I chose to tell him. And naturally I wouldn't do that—not while I was in my right mind! But it was embarrassing to have him think so well of me for not getting mad, when, actually, his being roped into visiting his grandparents was the best thing that could have happened to me.

I sighed. My feelings were too complicated to sort out at the moment. I tried to concentrate on the thought of Dick's phone call, which should be coming through almost any time now. But even the thought of that didn't make me feel as happy as it should have.

Chapter Four

I WRESTLE WITH A PROBLEM

ONCE I had talked to Dick I felt much better. That was to be expected, I suppose. And my family's wholehearted approval of my decision to go to Central for the big weekend also strengthened my morale. After all, I kept telling myself, it wasn't as if I were leaving Brose high and dry. He wouldn't even be around. Still I couldn't deny that I'd have felt happier about the whole deal if Brose knew of it and had said he didn't mind. On the other hand, if he knew of it and was as mad as I suspected he'd be, I'd feel even worse than I did. So I guessed it was best to let things ride.

Barbie Walters thought I was absolutely insane when I confided my doubts to her. This was on a Saturday morning and I had dropped in at the Walters' house just so I'd have someone to talk to—really talk, the way it's almost impossible to do with your parents. I know parents mean well, but they just don't understand things the way someone around your own age does.

"Jeepers!" Barbie said when I told her about Dick's invitation. "The most absolutely sensational things happen to you! Honestly, Tobey, I sometimes wonder if it's something about your aura or the sign of the zodiac you were born under or something. I mean you just seem to attract the unusual like—like—"

"Like flypaper attracts flies," I supplied drily.

"Well, yes, I suppose that covers it," Barbie said dreamily, taking off her glasses and polishing them with the ruffle of her peasant skirt. "But you really are lucky, you know. I mean, think of having Brose *and* being invited up to college by a man like Dick Allen."

I nodded. I couldn't deny I was lucky.

"And then," Barbie went on, "just so everything will run absolutely smoothly for you, fate steps in and makes

Brose have to go to Cleveland to visit his grandparents. I mean, if that isn't what you call leading a charmed life or something!" She sighed. "Now if it were me, things wouldn't work out like that. Oh, no! Sox would ask me out for the same nights and simply hit the ceiling when he found out I had a date with someone else. And then we'd have a big scrap and I'd be left with no local man at all—that's the way it'd be if someone asked me to a college dance."

"At least," I said, "if it worked out like that, Sox would know about it. You wouldn't have a horrible guilty feeling because you were keeping it all from him."

Barbie stared at me. Then she put her glasses on again, so she could stare at me even harder. "Don't tell me," she said, "your conscience is bothering you because Brose doesn't know!"

"Wouldn't yours, under the same circumstances?"

"Hah!" Barbie laughed in a very callous manner. "The way I see it, anything you can put over on a man, more power to you! I mean, look at the way they usually get away with murder and do their consciences ever bother them? No! In the battle of the sexes," Barbie said firmly, "quarter should neither be asked nor given. Besides, Brose doesn't own you, just remember that."

"I know," I admitted, "but we do have a sort of understanding."

"Even so," Barbie argued, "do you fondly imagine he'd sit around absolutely dateless if you were going to visit your grandparents and be gone several days?"

"He might," I said.

"Remember Mary Andrews," Barbie prodded brutally. "He didn't lose any time going to the Heart Hop with her when he got mad at you, did he?"

"But we're not mad now," I protested. "We're not mad a bit."

Barbie said thoughtfully, "And what was the name of that girl at the lake last summer, the one he went overboard for in a big way—she had such a sticky Southern accent—"

I remembered her name quite well—Kentucky Jackson. Just thinking of her and the way she had bewitched Brose for a little while made me mad all over again. But that wasn't fair, really. Because all that had been last summer and Brose had realized how foolish he had been, he had admitted it apologetically.

I said in an aloof sort of tone, "That's water under the bridge, Barbie. Let's not start swimming in it again at this late date."

"Okay," Barbie said mildly. "I only spoke of it so you'd see reason and not go getting any goofy ideas that you ought to tell Brose about your big date with Dick. I mean, can't you let well enough alone?"

"I suppose you're right," I said. Honestly, a conscience can be such a nuisance! Life would be much simpler if we were just born without one . . .

Still, even a smouldering sense of guilt can become such a familiar companion that we sort of forget about it. As the days passed and Thanksgiving week-end drew nearer, I found myself looking forward to it with scarcely a qualm. It was all going to be so different and exciting, such fun. Every time I thought of it, I felt flattered over Dick's having chosen me. And it wasn't as though I'd be slighting Brose by going. It wasn't even as though I liked Dick better than Brose. I didn't. I was quite sure of that.

Everything went on just as usual. School. And walking home with Brose and stopping in for sodas at Joe's. Going to the movies on Friday nights. Doing my own homework and helping Brose with his when he asked me to.

"Gee, you're a peach," he said one night in our living room after I'd seen him through a particularly tough French assignment.

We were sitting on the floor in front of the fireplace where a big log blazed and crackled. The November wind howled cold outside, but here it was warm and bright. Mom had brought us in a plate of cookies and some hot chocolate gooey with marshmallow a little while before. We were feeling full and relaxed.

"Why?" I asked. "What's so peachy about me? Aside, that is, from the fact that languages come easy for me."

"Well, that's one of your best points," Brose said judiciously. "And, of course, your mother makes awful good cookies."

"True," I said, flopping back on my elbows to grin at him. "But do you have to get so personal?"

"Oh, I could," Brose informed me. "If I wanted to break down. I could say, for intance, that the way your hair sort of glows in the firelight—well, it's almost exactly the color of copper pennies."

"Is it now?" I said lightly, although my heart was beating rather fast. Why, coming from Brose, anything so poetic as a comparison between my hair and copper pennies was almost overwhelming.

"Um-hum," Brose nodded. "And your eyes—well, they're sort of nice, too. Brown and—kind of sparkly. Warm-looking, that'd be the best description. Of course, the rest of your face is pretty bad. And your figure—" he made a clucking noise with his tongue and shook his head regretfully.

He ducked as I threw his French book at him and it landed on the floor with a dull thud. "Temper's bad, too," he said. "Takes a strong hand to keep you in order. And, brother, have I got the hand for it."

We were tussling then, laughing and clowning as we often do, like a couple of puppies, my father says. I got my hands into Brose's thick hair and pulled. But it was easy for him to pin both my arms at my sides with one of his. Then with the other hand he ruffled my hair down over my eyes, while he held me there, laughing and fuming and quite powerless to writhe out of his strong grip. My heart was hammering. It was sort of thrilling to be held so hard and close, without being hurt at all.

"You look like a sheep dog now," Brose teased, parting my hair with his fingers and peering through it at me.

Then he leaned closer and gave me a quick kiss and my heart hammered harder than ever. But I tried to wriggle out of his grip. When he still held me helpless, I took an

32

unfair feminine advantage. I said, "Brose, you're hurting me."

Immediately his hold on my arms relaxed and he said, his voice a little husky, "I'm sorry. I didn't mean to."

"That's okay," I chuckled. "You didn't really. I just thought it was time for recess."

"Yeah," Brose said. "Yeah, I guess so."

We sat there, laughing at each other, for a minute. Then Brose said, "I just thought of something else I like about you, another one of your good points."

"What?" I asked. "My hammerlock?"

"No, seriously," Brose said. "Just now you said I hurt you and then right away you admitted that I didn't really. You're pretty truthful, Tobey. That's a nice thing for a fella to know about his girl—that he can depend on her, on her word, I mean."

Suddenly I didn't feel like laughing any more. There was a lump the size of a baseball in my throat. I sat there, staring at Brose, thinking how wrong he was in his estimate of me. Honest? Why, I was deceiving him right this minute and had been for weeks. Ever since I'd accepted Dick's invitation and deliberately kept it from Brose. My eyes got wider and wider and the lump in my throat grew till I couldn't stand it any more. And suddenly with a little gulp I burst into tears and buried my face in my hands.

"Tobey," Brose was up on his knees beside me now, his big hands pulling at my shoulders awkwardly, his voice concerned. "What have I done? What's the matter? Gee, I'm sorry—"

I couldn't bear having him apologize when I was the one at fault. My tears fell faster than ever. Then Brose gathered me into his arms and I was crying against his shoulder, such a nice broad comfortable shoulder. And I could feel his hand smoothing back my hair and patting me soothingly. But I didn't deserve him. I didn't deserve anyone so wonderful at all.

When I could talk intelligibly, I told him all about everything. My face was still buried against his shoulder and he was still holding me close, so close I could feel his heart beating. But I expected him to shove me out of his arms any minute now that he knew about Dick and my plans to go up to Central for the week-end. I finished, "And I deceived you and kept it all from you, just because you're going to be away and probably wouldn't find out about it. And I've been feeling like an absolute louse."

"Fine thing!" Brose said gruffly. "Sneaking off with another guy behind my back. That's what it amounts to, isn't it?"

I nodded miserably. "I—guess so—but—" At least he hadn't pushed me away from him yet. I rubbed my cheek back and forth against the shoulder of his flannel shirt.

"Don't do that!" Brose snapped. "Trying to work on my feelings! What would you have done," he asked then, "if I hadn't been planning to go see my grandparents?"

"I was going to tell Dick I couldn't go," I explained. "And then before I had a chance to, you said you were going to Cleveland. So then I thought—I hoped maybe you wouldn't care, so long as you weren't even going to be here. And, oh, Brose, it sounds like such a wonderful week-end—and I've never been to a college dance—and I want to go so dreadfully."

"Because of the dance—or Dick?" Brose demanded.

I thought about it for a minute, wanting to be absolutely honest with him. "Because of the dance," I said then. "Oh, I won't say I don't like Dick at all. But no matter who asked me up to Central—so long as he wasn't absolutely revolting—I know I'd want to go."

"Hmmmm," Brose said. "You're sure?"

"Positive." I tipped my head back just far enough to get a good look at him.

Brose was scowling thoughtfully into space. "I suppose it isn't quite fair to expect you to turn down a date like that when I won't even be around to take you anywhere."

I didn't say anything. He sounded as though he was on

the right track. I figured it was safe to let him arrive at his destination under his own steam.

"On the other hand," Brose transferred his scowl from the distance to me, "I don't want you forgetting whose girl you are and getting all dazzled and starry-eyed over that twirp Allen."

"Of course I won't," I told him. This was no time to argue that Dick wasn't a twirp.

"Well—I guess it's okay then," Brose said gruffly. "But don't think I like it."

I smiled up at him, my absolutely most winning smile. "Gee, Brose, I think you're wonderful to take it like this. Really I do."

Brose grinned down at me. "Can't seem to stay mad at you, Tobey, no matter how good an excuse I've got."

"I'm glad," I told him. "And I feel ever so much better, now that you know all about it."

Brose's grin widened. "That's because you're what I said you were, back before the cloudburst. Honest. A guy can depend on you."

"You think so, even yet?" I asked.

And Brose said, "Sure. This only goes to prove it."

He was so sweet, standing there defending me in spite of the way I'd acted toward him, that the least I could do was reach up and give him a little kiss. Then Mom's voice in the hall made us scramble apart fast.

"It's after nine," Mom said from the doorway. "And tomorrow's a school day." This is my mother's tactful way of pointing out that it's time for Brose to go home, without coming right out and saying so. But on this particular occasion, I don't really think Brose would have noticed the difference, whatever she said.

As he straightened from picking up his French book, he said sort of dazedly, "I'm just going, Mrs. Heydon. Just going."

There was such a dreamy look on his face, I was afraid Mom would notice it as he passed her. But if she did, she didn't mention it.

Chapter Five

WEEK-END AT COLLEGE

I CERTAINLY wished, during the days that preceded the big week-end, that one of my older sisters was still around for me to consult. Both Janet and Alicia had gone to lots of college dances in their day, they could have given me loads of advice. As it was, I had to figure everything out for myself. Mom tried to help, but her ideas are pretty old-fashioned. And Barbie had never been to a college prom, neither had any of the other girls at school, so far as I knew, except Mary Andrews. And I wouldn't have asked her for advice under any circumstances.

Even Dad and Midge took a strong personal interest in the whole affair. Midge informed me solemnly that she had found out from Judy that red was Dick's favorite color. She seemed to think I should dash right out and buy myself a red dress. That would be all I needed, with my verging-on-red hair. But I tried to explain the unsuitability of the color tactfully, so that she wouldn't think I didn't appreciate her efforts in my behalf.

Dad offered no objection when I pointed out that I really should have a new formal for the occasion. I was a little worried about bringing the matter up. After all, he and Mom had bought me a new dress for the Heart Hop without my even asking. And it wasn't that the dress wasn't still perfectly good. But I had gone to the Heart Hop with Dick. And I would be going to this dance with him, too. And everyone knows you simply can't wear the same dress for two dances in a row and go with the same escort. Dad seemed a little confused when I explained this, still he didn't prove difficult to convince. Especially when Mom pointed out that if I got a new formal now, I'd be able to wear it for the Senior Prom at high school in the spring. Because I wouldn't be going to the prom with Dick, naturally. And none of my friends at school would have seen the new dress, so it would be perfectly all right.

Dad said wearily at this point, pressing his hand against his brow, "Please—just tell me how much money you need and let it go at that. Trying to follow a woman's logic is like going on a scavenger hunt with all the clues written in disappearing ink."

Mom spoke thoughtfully to me, ignoring my father, "Will your navy faille do for the party at Dick's fraternity house? And I suppose you'll wear your gray suit for the game—or maybe your plaid wool?"

"My plaid wool's a rag," I said, shaking my head regretfully. "But my suit's okay—only I thought maybe a new blouse would sort of pep it up. I should think my navy would do, unless—"

"Fifty dollars," my father interrupted in a firm voice, "is my absolute top. You two may spend that much in any way you see fit. Beyond that I will not go."

"Oh, Henry," Mom said reproachfully, "don't go issuing an ultimatum. You know we'll keep it down just as low as possible."

And we did. Even Dad was impressed with my formal, aqua, with one of those swoony wired bodices that stay up without straps, and yards and yards of skirt to swirl gracefully as I danced. With it I would wear my long black gloves, black ballet slippers, and a black velvet ribbon around my neck. It is a strange phenomenon, but every male I know seems to go for this black velvet ribbon thing in a big way. So who am I to fight against what seems to be a natural weakness?

Mom let me buy a new blouse, too, and a little velvet cap to wear on the back of my head. But even so, we didn't go much over the amount Dad had mentioned and he was agreeably surprised.

All my girl friends drooled enviously over my new clothes. But most of all they envied me my date for a college dance. Every one of them wished it were she who was going. And they made me promise to remember every single detail so that I could tell them all about it later. As if I ever intended to forget!

Dick had explained the second time he phoned me that off-campus dates were to be put up at various sorority houses. He had arranged for me to stay with the girl who was going to the dance with his roommate. Her name was Geraldine Clair and she was a Theta. It all sounded so terribly exciting and thrilling I could hardly eat a bite of Thanksgiving dinner Thursday for thinking about it. I had seen Brose for a little while Wednesday afternoon, just before he was ready to leave for Cleveland. He was looking so glum my heart went out to him and I assured him I'd ever so much rather be going to a college week-end with him. This cheered him a little, but not much.

He said, "We can't even look forward to that. With me going halfway across the country next fall to college, I'll be lucky if I get to see you a couple of times a year."

Brose's father went to Colorado to college and he has his mind made up that Brose must go there, too. And Brose wouldn't care except that it means leaving me for such long periods of time. His attitude is really very flattering and I know I'll miss him, too, but just at the moment I wasn't in a brooding mood.

"I know," I said, but I couldn't seem to keep the lilt out of my voice.

"Please," Brose said. "Must you sound so happy about it?"

He grinned then and patted my hand. "It's okay. I know how het up you are over this week-end. But just don't have too good a time with that claim-jumper. Remember whose girl you are."

"I will," I told him. "I won't forget for a minute."

And I wouldn't. But I'd have to admit my feet scarcely touched the ground when I walked, I was that excited and filled with anticipation . . .

The trip to Central University by train is a comparatively short one. All the way I kept studying the other girls in my coach, wondering how many of them were headed for the same destination. It seemed to me that every one of the likely ones looked ever so much smoother and more poised and sophisticated than I. Older, too.

And although I kept telling myself this was only imagination on my part, I felt my self-confidence begin to curl up into a little weensy shred inside of me, like a twist of dried-up orange peel. My gray suit and the smart new blouse and hat that had seemed so satisfactory at home didn't do a thing for me now. Why had I ever said I'd go, I wondered? Why had I thought it would be fun to compete with a lot of beautiful glamorous girls with gorgeous clothes and so much self-assurance it positively oozed from them? I felt that my nose was shiny and my lipstick smeared and probably my stocking seams weren't even straight. Or my slip could be showing.

What would I say to Dick when I saw him, what would we have to talk about? Within five minutes he'd probably be sorry he had ever invited me to come.

At this point my common sense, of which, thank goodness, I have at least an average amount, came to my rescue. See here, Tobey Heydon, it said firmly, don't go getting into a complete tizzy. This isn't any blind date, you know. Dick didn't ask you up to college sight unseen. You didn't have any trouble talking to him the night of the Heart Hop and you were complete strangers then, hadn't even laid eyes on each other before. Why do you imagine this week-end will be different? And as for your looks and your clothes, nobody's ever complained about them so far. Brose has always seemed satisfied, hasn't he? Well, then!

I began sort of studying some of the other girls in the coach. The blonde in green, for instance. Actually I didn't like her hat so well as mine. And the way she fussed with her hair every now and then made me wonder if she was feeling any more sure of herself than I was. And the brunette in red definitely had on too much eye shadow —it gave her an artificial look. Both girls were pretty, true, but I'd be willing to bet they might be suffering a qualm or two over the week-end ahead. Like me they were probably wondering whether they'd have fun and be popular, if the boys they were going to meet would be flatteringly attentive, if it was all going to be as wonderful as they imagined.

A little smile curled up my mouth and the blond girl, happening to glance my way just then, smiled, too, a trifle hesitantly. Then we both looked away in the self-conscious way people on trains always seem to. But I didn't feel so worried any more. After all, I reminded myself, Dick asked you to come and nobody stood over him with a big club to make him. Just keep that in mind and don't let your imagination run away with you and everything will be just fine.

The minute I laid eyes on Dick, waiting for me on the station platform, I felt the last of my silly fears wilt away. For one thing he was even better looking than I remembered, tallish and with smooth dark hair and a nice smile. His clothes were casual without being sloppy in that wonderful way that college men have. And he welcomed me so warmly and introduced me with such enthusiasm to all his friends we happened to encounter, that I felt thrilled and flattered and so happy I practically glowed.

We rode out to the sorority house, where I was to stay, in a swoony convertible, which, Dick explained, he had borrowed in order to impress me. He said, "Can't risk letting you ride in one of the local taxis, Tobey. I want you in good shape for the party tonight."

"What kind of party will it be, Dick?" I asked.

"Oh, just a plain little old session of the brothers and their women—chance to get acquainted and all that."

The Theta house was southern colonial, with tall pillars and lots of charm. Dick came into the living room and stayed with me till Geraldine Clair, whom everyone called Geri, came down to welcome me. She was a slim blond girl with a comfortable personality and right away I liked her.

As I told Dick good-bye, he murmured, pressing my hand, "Don't look at me like that now. Save all those stars in your eyes till I come back to take you out to dinner. See you at six."

Honestly, I don't think any girl could have a more perfectly wonderful week-end than this one seemed to be shaping into. Geri Clair and I got to be good friends in a very short time, helping each other dress and borrowing cold cream and nail polish and stuff. Geri was able to give me ever so many pointers as to what to wear and how to act. We sort of operated on my navy faille, making the neckline slightly more plunging and tucking a red flower of Geri's into it for effect. And I loaned her my nylon blouse to wear with a black velvet skirt of hers and honestly, if we did say it as shouldn't, we were two of the best dressed girls at the party that night.

It was ever so much fun. When Dick and I got to his fraternity house after an elegant dinner, the bum room was already beginning to get crowded. Before long you could hardly move, but no one minded. Someone played the piano and lots of people sang and some danced, if you could call worming your way through that genial mob dancing. Some of the brothers put on a perfectly screaming skit in which Dick was a hula girl in a grass skirt with a hibiscus flower behind his ear and Geri's Charlie Curtin was a native chieftain with hay fever. We nearly died laughing.

Then there was a wonderful buffet supper, but we all went out for hamburgers and stuff later on just the same. I guess going to college doesn't impair people's appetites a bit.

Dick and I and Geri and Charlie strolled back to the sorority house through the frosty moonlight, our breath clouding before us in the clear cold air. My hand was warm in Dick's. Geri and Charlie were a few steps ahead of us, intent on their own conversation. I sighed.

"Aren't you having fun?" Dick asked a shade anxiously.

"Oh, yes. I just sighed because I'm happy," I told him. "It's all so wonderful."

"You're the one who's wonderful," Dick said softly. He said then, fingering Brose's class ring, "I hope I didn't make difficulties for you with—whoever this belongs to. It's new since I saw you last, isn't it?"

I nodded. "He wasn't too mad, though." I explained about Brose going to Cleveland and all.

"Lucky break for me," Dick said, squeezing my hand a little tighter.

"Me, too," I admitted. "You see, I've never been to a college dance before."

"It doesn't show a bit," Dick said. Did I imagine it, or did he sound ever so slightly embarrassed, uncomfortable? I must have imagined it, I decided, as he went on, "We couldn't have picked a better dance for you to begin on than the Inter-Fraternity. It's always quite a plushy affair." He proceeded to tell me a little about it, describing the hotel ballroom in which it was to be held, the orchestra that had been secured for it, the decorative theme. It sounded swoony.

We were almost back to Geri's sorority house when I suddenly remembered something. I told Dick, "I called Alicia earlier this evening, just to say hello and let her know I was here."

"Oh, yes," Dick remembered, "your sister. Married to a pre-med, isn't she?"

I nodded. "Adam Wentworth. They live in Quonset Village. Alicia asked us over for breakfast, if you think we'd have time, with the game tomorrow afternoon and all."

"Why, sure," Dick agreed. "I'd like very much to meet them." He chuckled. "Like to see the inside of one of those quonsets, too. They intrigue me."

I hadn't seen Alicia's and Adam's home yet, either. So the next morning they showed us hospitably around the little place before we sat down to breakfast. It didn't take long, I must admit, but it was really quite cute. Alicia had done wonders with plaid gingham and bright shag rugs. And she and Adam were so obviously happy, so much in love, it lent everything around them a sort of special glow. Both of them seemed ever so much more agreeable than they used to before they were married. Alicia and I had always tangled a lot at home and I have had some dillies of scraps with Adam, too. But this morning they couldn't have been sweeter. It was easy to see that Dick liked them both very much.

Breakfast was delicious, waffles and pork sausages. Alicia had actually learned how to cook. She even looked prettier than she used to. Her sort of pale blondness had more zip and sparkle now. Marriage certainly became her.

After we had eaten, Dick and Adam got into a discussion of Central's chances against Dundee in the game that afternoon. I helped Alicia carry the dishes out to her phone-booth size kitchen.

"I like your new man," she confided under cover of our clatter. "He's a great improvement over Brose Gilman."

I felt myself bristling. I guess Alicia could be just as annoying as ever when she put her mind on it. I said coldly, "Dick is very nice, but I still like Brose, too." And I held up my finger with his class ring on it for her to see.

"Oh, no!" Alicia's smile was pitying. "I thought you'd outgrown that sort of thing." She made me sound as if I were all of Midge's age and I felt myself flushing with anger. But, after all, we couldn't have a quarrel right in front of Dick.

So I said merely, keeping my voice low with an effort, "It really isn't any affair of yours."

Alicia laughed, so I guess marriage has improved her sense of humor, anyway. "So it isn't," she said, dropping the touchy subject. And she proceeded to ask me what I was going to wear to the dance that night. And by the time I had told her and she had described her new formal for me, we had the dishes done and were all friendly again, with no hard feelings at all.

Chapter Six

THE DANCE—AND DISILLUSIONMENT!

THE REST of the day whirled past like one of those trick movie shots that show a lot of things happening, all sort of merging into one another. The weather wasn't too good, rather gray and muggy, but it didn't actually rain. Central lost the game by one field goal, but, although I pretended to feel sad about it for Dick's sake, I didn't really care too much. It was all colorful and exciting anyway, the big stadium packed with cheering crowds, the band playing college songs on the field between halves, the cheer leaders knocking themselves out as though they loved it.

One rather odd thing happened, but I didn't think much about it at the time. It was between quarters and Dick and I were eating hot dogs and drinking Cokes, when a sandy-haired young man, approaching down the aisle on the other side of Dick, hailed him cheerfully, "Hi, Dick!" he exclaimed, clapping him on the shoulder, then, to me, "Hi, Kay." He got a better look at me then and an expression of ludicrous embarrassment passed across his face.

"Ooops, sorry," he said.

Dick flushed a little, introducing us, and after a few minutes of slightly stilted conversation, the sandy-haired young man hurried on his way.

I couldn't resist the temptation to tease Dick a bit. "Who is this Kay he took me for?"

"Oh, just a girl I know," Dick explained, his color still a little high. "Kay Delafield, her name is. But I can't imagine why he confused you with her. You don't look anything alike. Besides—"

The whistle blew just then, so we didn't discuss the matter any further. I got the impression that Dick was glad of the interruption, but I couldn't see why. Surely he didn't think I'd be jealous, did he? On the contrary, I felt more flattered than ever that he'd asked me to Central for the week-end when he had a girl right here on campus he could have dated.

After the game we joined a crowd of Dick's fraternity brothers and their girls at the Student Union, where we sat around talking about everything in the world and drinking Cokes and sodas. It was all gay and noisy and lots of fun. Half a dozen of us had dinner together at a place called the Barn, which was a favorite campus hang-out. Right afterwards Geri Clair and I made Charlie Curtin and Dick take us back to the Theta house. We wanted to allow ourselves plenty of time to dress for the dance, because we knew what a madhouse it would be with a lot of extra girls under the same roof and all getting ready for a big evening.

And it was! You never saw such a rush and confusion, such tearing around half dressed, such congestion at the showers, such borrowing of nail polish and bobby pins. Poor Mrs. Carpenter, the house mother, did her best to help us all, but we had her going around in circles in no time. Still she remained good-humored throughout all the upheaval, which was more than some women would have been capable of. I imagine, though, she was going to be pretty relieved when the big week-end was over and things got back to normal around the sorority house.

My dress looked really sensational with my long black gloves and the little velvet ribbon around my throat. Dick's corsage I had to tuck in my hair, since the strapless top of my dress afforded little anchoring space for flowers. Geri's dress was black and even more sophisticated than mine. We each assured the other earnestly that she looked perfectly marvelous.

Then I asked, just a shade doubtfully, "You don't think I look too—too young, do you?" Some of the other dresses I had glimpsed in the hall made mine seem a trifle ingénue.

Geri shook her head positively. "You look sweet, pet. Dick'll love you. You'll make a wonderful contrast to some of these junior grade Mata Haris."

A memory struck me then and I asked Geri, "You don't happen to know a girl named Kay Delafield, do you?"

Geri's blue eyes sort of slid away from mine and she began brushing at the skirt of her dress as though there was a bit of lint on it, although I couldn't see a thing. "Kay Delafield?" she repeated. "Why—yes, I know her slightly."

"She's a friend of Dick's," I prompted.

"Who told you about her?" Geri asked.

"No one, really," I admitted. "Somebody took me for

45

her at the game, but when I asked Dick about her, all he said was that we didn't look a bit alike."

"Dick's right, you don't." Geri's eyes came up to meet mine. "I wouldn't give her another thought if I were you."

Geri's manner mystified me a little, just as Dick's had. I said, "I'm not jealous for pity's sake. Dick invited me to the dance of his own free will, which must mean he wanted me. If he preferred to take Kay Delafield, he'd have asked her."

"Of course," Geri agreed instantly. "That's exactly the way to look at it. You're so right, pet . . ."

Dick's glance kindled in a most satisfactory way as I came down the stairs to join him a little later. The hall was simply milling with people, but he managed to whisper, "You're terrific," as he helped me on with my coat. Then we were outside with Geri and Charlie in the dark chilly night, climbing into Charlie's car, talking and laughing. Excitement rose in me like gingerale bubbles.

The hotel ballroom had been transformed into a snow-shrouded forest, pine trees sprinkled with silver all about, synthetic drifts around the edge of the dance floor, soft blue lights giving it all an eerie enchanting effect. No girl could have asked for a more attentive escort than Dick. He had swapped a few of my dances with fraternity brothers, but only, he informed me, because he couldn't avoid it gracefully.

"I'd rather have you all to myself," he confided, his lips close to my ear as we danced to the dreamy music. The way he looked at me was enough to go to any girl's head. I felt my heart beat faster under my strapless bodice. And then I thought about poor Brose, far away in Cleveland hobnobbing with his grandparents, and felt a little ashamed of myself for having such a wonderful time. But I couldn't keep that up very long.

Quite late in the evening the crowning of the Prom Queen and King was scheduled.

"Who will they be?" I asked Dick. "Or is it hush-hush?"

Dick said a trifle grimly, "One of those secrets everybody knows. The King's a Big Wheel named Forrester—Brad Forrester. The Queen's Kay Delafield."

"She is?" I must have sounded rather startled. I certainly felt that way. I said then, "I had no idea she was so sensational."

"She's not," Dick said. "A lot of politics enter into a selection like that. A lot of wires get pulled. Oh, I don't mean to imply Kay's hard to look at or anything. But there are dozens of girls at Central just as easy on the eyes." He grinned down at me and maybe I just imagined that grin took some effort. "You're as pretty as she any day."

"Thanks," I said and felt his hand close around mine. "Point her out to me, will you?"

Dick's frowning glance swept the room. After a minute he said. "She's dancing near the orchestra—dark hair, white formal—that's to match her imitation ermine robe later."

"Gleeps!" I said, my eyes widening. "She certainly *is* terrific."

"Matter of taste," Dick said shortly. "Personally, there are other types I like much better." He squeezed my hand hard. "Only for heaven's sake, can't we talk about something else now?"

It seemed to me there was a sort of desperate note in his voice. So I said soothingly, "Why, of course, Dick. Anything you like . . ."

But somehow, no matter what we talked about, or how well we danced together, my mind kept drifting back to that tall gorgeous brunette in the stark white formal. Dick had sounded so bitter about her—but why? Evidently they had been good enough friends so that the sandy-haired boy at the game had automatically taken me for Kay, just because I was with Dick. That sounded as though they were a fairly solid twosome. Why, then, hadn't Dick asked her to the dance instead of me? All that talk of his about student politics, about wires being pulled to elect her Prom Queen—did that have something to do with it? Maybe, I thought, they had quarreled and Dick had asked someone else to the dance to make Kay jealous.

Maybe his flattering attention to me all evening was for that purpose, too. But that was silly, I told myself. It wasn't as if I'd been asked at the last minute. Dick had called me weeks ago. I was simply getting into a tizzy over nothing.

I tried to dismiss the entire matter from my mind. But my head seemed to be full of jigsaw-puzzle pieces that wouldn't quite fit together. I wasn't even sure I wanted to find the missing key piece. Maybe I wouldn't like it when I did.

We ran into Alicia and Adam in the press of people and Dick and Adam swapped partners for one dance. Just as I remembered, Adam was a lousy dancer. No sooner was I back with Dick again than it was time for the crowning.

Kay Delafield made a spectacular Queen in her robes and glittering crown and scepter. Enthroned beside blond handsome Brad Forrester, surrounded by their attendants, she was breath-taking. But Dick's scowl was so ferocious, I didn't dare say so. And he kept muttering, "I wish they'd get through with all this hoop-la, so we can dance."

Later, when the crowd had begun to thin out a little, we decided to go to the Barn for an after-the-dance snack with Geri and Charlie. Geri and I went to fix our faces and it was in the powder room, quite unexpectedly, that a couple of perfect strangers, gossiping in front of the long mirror, supplied me with the missing piece of my jigsaw. They were discussing Kay and how lucky she had been to be chosen Prom Queen.

"She's not having too sharp a time, though," one of the girls confided to the other. "The Delts are boycotting her to a man and they're about the smoothest fraternity on campus."

I couldn't help pricking up my ears. Naturally, I felt curious as to why Dick's fraternity would boycott Kay.

Geri tugged urgently at my elbow. "Ready, pet?"

But I shook my head and listened unashamedly to the neighboring conversation, which was beginning to get very interesting indeed. The other girl having asked, "Why should the Delts boycott her?" the first girl an-

48

swered, "Haven't you heard? She said she'd go to the dance with one of them and then, when she saw she had a chance to get elected Queen by being sweet to Brad Forrester and his crowd, she gave her Delt date the boot. And less than a month before the dance, too—and you know how it is with the Inter-Fraternity, dates are set months ahead, or you get strictly what's left over, or else import somebody—"

There was more, but I let Geri draw me away then. I'd heard enough. My throat ached and I felt hot tears sting behind my lashes. So I was strictly from desperation, someone Dick had thought of when he was in a spot and wanted to save his pride. And I had felt so flattered, so pleased that he had chosen me. I'd been stupid, that was what hurt, not realizing I was second choice.

Geri said softly, her hand on my shoulder, "Tobey, I'm sorry—so sorry you heard that."

"Why?" I asked, blinking a little, but not shedding a tear. "I was almost sure to catch on sooner or later."

"Tobey," Geri said, very woman-to-woman, "listen to me. There's no reason at all to let this spoil things for you."

"Everything's pretty spoiled now," I said wryly. "I—suppose Dick figured I was so—so young and silly I wouldn't realize I was being invited awfully late for a big dance. And he was so right. I didn't realize it. I felt—flattered—" my voice wobbled dangerously.

Geri's hand pressed my shoulder. "Well, there wasn't anything unflattering about it," she argued. "Dick was pretty much on a spot. His girl here at college had stood him up in a way that isn't easy for the male ego to take. So he casts about in his mind for somebody who'll stand out, who'll show Kay she's by no means indispensable. And he invites you. Sure, you're second choice, but under the circumstances that's not such a bad thing to be. It proves Dick likes you a lot, that he thinks you're more than slightly sensational. And he's certainly done everything he could to give you a wonderful week-end."

"Well—yes—" I had to admit that what Geri was saying made sense. "But—everyone knows about it."

"Oh, come now," Geri reasoned with me. "Central's a big college, you know. Dick's fraternity brothers are in on it—but they're all on your side. You heard what those girls said about them boycotting Kay."

"But those girls—" I sniffed, "they knew."

"Maybe a handful of people out of all this mob," Geri admitted. "And you notice those girls didn't know names —they merely said Kay had double-crossed 'some Delt.' That covers a lot of ground. So what? So who cares?" Her blue eyes were pleading. "If only you won't feel you have to make a *thing* of it, when Dick's tried so hard to show you a grand time, when he's having so much fun himself in spite of that louse Kay Delafield."

I asked, not feeling quite so bad as I had a few minutes before, "You really think he is?"

"Of course," Geri said positively. "Can't you tell?"

"I thought so," I admitted. "Now I wonder if he's just pretending."

"He's not that good an actor," Geri said, chuckling.

Rather to my own surprise, I found myself smiling, too. The hurt was still there, down underneath, but as yet it was a purely personal hurt, involving no one else but me. If I told Dick what I'd overheard, he'd be miserable, too. And what good would it do, really? As Geri had pointed out, we were having a grand time. Dick wasn't just pretending, I felt sure of it. I'd made him forget his hurt over Kay, to some extent anyway. And if we got into a big discussion of his reason for asking me to the dance, it would only spoil things for both of us, leave a bad taste in our mouths when we looked back on this whole week-end later on. Why not, my common sense demanded in its most common sensible manner, let well enough alone?

I said tentatively to Geri, "You think it would be smart to make like I hadn't heard a word back there in the powder room?"

She nodded. "I think it would be very smart."

"I'll do it," I said, reaching a sudden decision. Geri gave me a quick little hug of approval.

So we joined the boys quite as though nothing had happened and went on to the Barn for hamburgers and malteds and a lot of rambling silly wonderful talk. Afterwards, saying good-night on the moon-dappled porch of the Theta house, Dick told me, "Tobey, you're swell. I can't remember a week-end that's been more fun."

"Really, Dick?" I asked softly. I was awfully glad I'd taken Geri's advice.

"Absolutely," Dick said, his arm tightening thrillingly around my waist. His voice was a little husky, asking, "Tobey, what about this class ring you're wearing? Are you serious about him?"

It was a little hard to remember Brose clearly, with Dick so close. But I tried and finally his face came clear in my mind, his nice familiar face. I said, "We're—very fond of each other, very good friends."

Dick spoke firmly. "I mean to give him some stiff competition when I get back to Edgewood. Do you mind?"

I felt my heart beat faster. I wouldn't mind. But Brose would. Oh, definitely! It was going to be fun. I said demurely, "We'll see—when you get back to Edgewood."

Dick's lips touched my cheek. He would have kissed my mouth if I hadn't turned my head at the last minute. It took considerable effort on my part. But it seemed like the least I could do for Brose . . .

Chapter Seven

HOLIDAYS AHEAD

I GUESS there are times in every girl's life when she finds it necessary—not to lie exactly, but not to tell quite the whole truth, either. Going home on the train Sunday, I had time to figure out just what part of the week-end I was going to build up and what part had better be toned down a little in my recital of events. Mom would ask a lot of questions. So would Barbie and all my other girl friends. Brose would be curious, too. And I intended to answer their questions, but I didn't mean to mention Kay Delafield, or the fact that Dick's invitation to me had been definitely an after-thought. Why should I? It would be so much easier on my pride to draw a veil over the unpleasant aspects of the week-end. And a girl has a right to a few secrets.

So when Mom and Dad and Midge wanted to know all about everything, I filled in details till they couldn't ask for more. I told them about the party at the Delt house and the game and the dance that had climaxed the week-end. I told them about having had breakfast with Alicia and Adam, described their cute little home, dwelt on how well they were getting along and how happy they were and delivered all the messages they had given me. I told about Geri Clair and how congenial we had been, what fun Dick and I had had with her and Charlie Curtin.

Mom beamed at me and said, "I'm so glad you had a wonderful time, darling."

And Dad asked, beaming a little, too, "Why shouldn't she with all those elegant new clothes you two put the bite on me for?"

Mom shook her head. "Clothes don't always mean fun. I had the most terrible time once at a dance in a perfectly beautiful pink georgette dress. My escort stepped on my ruffles and I lost my petticoat right on the dance floor."

Midge went off into gales of laughter at the notion of such a slapstick comedy disaster. She gasped between giggles, "Mom, you didn't! Couldn't you have just died?"

"I wished at the time I could," Mom admitted. "But nothing so convenient happened. I had to step out of my petticoat, pick it up and run for the girls' room. And my escort simply stood there blushing. I never forgave him."

"Was it Daddy?" Midge asked.

"Of course *not!*" Mom said. "You think I could marry a man who had done a thing like that to me?"

"Was it Gordon Detwiler?" Dad asked, sort of rolling the syllables around on his tongue.

Mom gave him a nasty look. "It was long after Gordon left Edgewood," she said reprovingly. "This was a boy I never liked very well anyway. He was visiting Jody Peterson—he was her cousin. And we had this double date—just one. I could never bear the sight of him after that."

"You never told us about that before," I said to Mom.

And Dad said, "She never even told me."

Mom shook her head, smiling just a little. "For a long time I couldn't bear to think of it myself—I tried to wall it off in my mind and pretend it hadn't happened. But—" her smile widened, "I guess it's true that time heals all things. Now it merely seems funny to me."

I wondered whether sometime I might tell my children and husband about the time I'd got invited to a big college week-end and hadn't had the sense to realize I was second choice? Already the hurt of it seemed to be dulling a little.

Dad said, "But isn't it unreasonable to hate the poor guy for something that was obviously an accident? You surely don't feel he stepped on your skirt on purpose."

Mom said, "He had no right to be so clumsy. Anyway, it happened a good twenty-five years ago, so let's not get all sorry for him at this late date. I'm sure he's led a happy normal life in spite of my dislike." She turned to me then, apparently dismissing Jody Peterson's clumsy cousin from her mind. "Tobey, were Alicia and Adam at the dance, too?"

I nodded. "Alicia looked sensational. She had on rose velvet with the bodice sort of shaped like petals at the top, very becoming."

We went on talking about the dance until the phone rang. Midge and I raced for it and I won, for a change. It was Brose, just as I had hoped it would be. I signaled Midge to scram.

He had got home from Cleveland only a few minutes before and he wanted me to go for a walk. My heart bumped happily. I realized I hadn't seen him for four whole days.

We went for a long walk through streets that were just turning a lovely blue with dusk. Brose held my hand tight and it felt right at home. We had ever so much to talk about and yet there were long intervals when we simply strolled along, our shoulders touching, not saying anything, not needing to.

Once Brose asked, "Was it all as wonderful as you expected, Tobey?"

And I answered, "Well—practically. Why?"

He said, "Oh, I was kind of hoping something wouldn't be so terrific about it. Selfish of me, I guess."

"Human, too, though," I said, smiling up at him. Even if I wasn't going to tell him the whole truth about the week-end, I didn't want him feeling too glum about it. I said softly, "We've had some wonderful dates, too."

"Sure," Brose brightened, "we have, at that. And there'll be a lot more, too, what with the holidays coming and the Senior Prom in the spring."

I sighed happily. Hearing Brose talk that way gave me a nice warm safe feeling. No question of my being anything but first with him. And he was first with me, I assured myself. Of course, I liked Dick a lot, too. It bothered me a little to realize I could be so fond of two boys at the same time. Did other girls sometimes have this queer uncertain feeling, as if they were being pulled two ways at once? But I did like Brose best. I was sure of it—or almost sure.

His voice broke into my thoughts urgently. "Tobey, I don't want you chasing off with Dick Allen again. If I hadn't been going to Cleveland, I'd have raised Cain this time."

"If you hadn't been going," I soothed him, "I'd have told Dick I wouldn't come." At least, I was pretty sure I would have.

"Gee, Tobey," Brose's voice was husky, "I thought about you all the time I was away. I wondered what you were doing, whether you were—getting too interested in that guy Allen." His tone got worried then. "You—you didn't, did you?"

"Of course not," I said as matter-of-factly as I could. "Oh, Dick's nice. He showed me a wonderful time, but—well, I'm still wearing your ring."

"Yeah," Brose said, "I know." He asked then, chuckling, "What did he have to say about it—the ring, I mean?"

"Oh, he wanted to know whose it was and how long I'd had it—stuff like that."

"And you told him?"

I nodded. "Of course."

"What did he say then?"

I looked up at Brose, my heart beating just a little faster. "You really want to know?"

"Naturally I want to know," Brose said, frowning.

"Well, Dick said that when he got back to Edgewood, he was going to give you some stiff competition."

"Oh, he did, did he?" Brose growled. Suddenly he stopped walking and stared down at me narrowly. "Tobey, will you tell me the absolute truth about something?"

"Why—I'll try, Brose." I made my eyes wide and innocent, having a pretty good idea what was coming.

"Did he—" Brose sort of gulped, "did he kiss you?"

I shook my head. "N-no—that is, not exactly."

"What do you mean by that?" Brose's scowl made little shivers quiver down my spine.

I admitted softly, "He tried—but I didn't let him."

"The louse!" Brose said. "The stinker!" Then his hand closed more tightly around mine and his voice got gentle again as we strolled on slowly through the chill twilight. "I should have known I could depend on you."

"Of course," I agreed. But I wondered if he'd have felt quite so sure about it if he had known the effort it had taken to turn my cheek to Dick Allen's lips ...

Once Thanksgiving is past, it always seems as if the days simply race along until Christmas. And this year was no exception. For one thing, I was swamped with school work. In addition to doing my own, I was helping Brose with his French, since we couldn't let him flunk a subject in his Senior year. Then there was shopping to do, cards to write, all the lovely confusion that the approach of the holidays brings on.

Mom said, in a tone of rather wistful regret, "It won't seem like Christmas, really, with no children in the house who believe in Santa Claus.".

I knew she was remembering last year. It had been hectic, but fun, with my older sister Janet and her little boy, Toots, staying with us. All the Christmas preparations had to be kept secret from Toots, who was only three then. Adam Wentworth had been pressed into impersonating Santa Claus for Toots's benefit. Adam hadn't been too willing, but Alicia worked on him—they weren't married at that time and she had the poor guy wrapped around her little finger. And then at the last minute on Christmas Eve, Janet's husband, Jim Clark, had turned up from Panama to surprise us all. Any Christmas was bound to seem like an anticlimax after that one.

I comforted Mom, "At least, we won't have to watch our tongues the way we did last year. It's a wonder Toots didn't get his young illusions trampled on, as it was."

Mom said gently, her eyes suspiciously moist, "Dear little Toots—Janet says they're calling him Jimmy nowadays, because that nickname seems too babyish. Oh, I wish they hadn't gone all the way out to California to live!"

I suppose it is a little rough on grandmothers, when some of their family move so far away. And now with Janet expecting another baby around the first of the year, there was no possibility of their getting back to visit us for ages.

"It could be worse," I reminded Mom. "What if they'd gone to Guatemala, as they thought they might have to for a while?"

"That's the trouble with marrying an engineer," Mom said. "It's so unsettling."

"Sort of romantic, though," I said dreamily. "Faraway places, strange people—"

"Bad water," Mom put in, "heat, flies."

"Well, yes, I suppose so," I had to admit.

"No suppose about it," Mom said in an irritated sort of way that wasn't at all like her. "You know perfectly well how afraid they were to take Toots—Jimmy," she corrected herself, "to Central America when Jim was working down there."

I said soothingly, "But that's all over now. They're perfectly fine out in California."

"How do we know?" Mom asked, a little worried frown between her eyes. "It's so far away and Janet's just like me about writing letters. Sometimes we don't hear from them for weeks. She claims she has a competent woman lined up to take care of Jimmy while she's in the hospital and to help with the new baby—but—well, I'd feel a lot better if they were close enough so I could see about things first hand."

I patted her shoulder soothingly. "Never mind, Mom. When I get married I'll live real close. And I'll bring all my children over every day for you to take care of. You'll be knee-deep in grandchildren."

Mom smiled a little then. "I suppose I am being silly. It's just that it would be so wonderful if we could all be together for Christmas—only I know we can't."

"You've still got Midge and Dad and me," I reminded her. "And Alicia and Adam will be here Christmas Eve."

Adam had an elderly, rather eccentric aunt, Miss Tess Wentworth, with whom he and his father always spent Christmas Day. Now that Alicia was married to Adam, she'd have to go to his aunt's house, too. But since we celebrated on Christmas Eve, it wouldn't disrupt our plans.

"I know," Mom said, "and it's only a little over a week off. I don't really have time to get all sentimental and morbid, with so much left to do. I haven't finished wrapping presents and there are cookies still to bake and the decorations to get down from the attic. I wonder," she said thoughtfully, "if I shouldn't have Dad check on the tree lights and be sure we've got plenty."

I could tell by the intent gleam in her eye that she had started thinking along more constructive lines than futile regrets over the absence of Janet and Toots. So I let my mind drift into a bit of pleasant daydreaming of my own. I wondered what Brose was getting me for Christmas—I wondered what everybody was getting me. And then the lovely thought of Dick Allen being home for the holidays crowded my speculations about gifts aside. If Dick paid much attention to me, Brose would be fit to be tied. And Dick had said— A delicious little shiver wiggled through me at the memory of all Dick had said. Christmas was always fun, but I had an idea it might be even more sensational than usual this year.

Chapter Eight

MIDGE HAS AN IDEA

MIDGE is an odd little twirp in some ways. She seems so completely open and uncomplicated and then all of a sudden she does something that makes you realize there are unexplored depths in her nature. I suppose everybody's like that, but in a ten-year-old it seems a little startling.

A few days before Christmas, she came into my bedroom where I was wrapping presents. Fortunately I wasn't working on one of hers. I had just finished tying a really impressive silver bow on the package containing the Argyle sox I had knitted for Brose. Or rather, I had started knitting them and Mom had finished them for me. I guess she has a calmer nature than I. All those little dangling bobbins of different colored yarn simply drove me crazy, but they didn't bother Mom a bit. In fact, she got so enthralled with knitting Argyles, that she did a pair for my father, too, although I don't really think he is quite a dashing enough type to do justice to them. But they will be wonderful for Brose and he will appreciate all the work I put into them ever so much.

I doubt that he will appreciate the time and ribbon I lavished on wrapping his gift, however. Men aren't ever very observant about things like that. But I love to do it, so I started sticking silver stars on the dark green paper, the while I gave my little sister a rather dirty look.

"You might knock," I reminded her. "I could just as well have been wrapping your present, you know."

Midge shook her head. "You wrapped it a coupl'a days ago, remember? I started to come in and you yelled real loud at me and made me go 'way till you had time to hide it."

"Someday you'll get into trouble snooping," I warned.

But Midge denied, "I don't really snoop. It's just that I like to go 'round in my stocking-feet. But I wouldn't ackshully want to see any of my presents ahead of time. It's more fun to be surprised Christmas Eve." She asked then, plopping herself down on the foot of my bed, just missing all my fancy wrapping paper, "I s'pose that's for Brose? You wouldn't waste so much ribbon on any of the fam'ly."

"Oh, I wouldn't say that." But I admitted this was Brose's gift. I stuck on another silver star for good measure.

"You giving him anything besides those sox?" Midge asked.

I nodded. "I'm not going to tell you what, though."

"Oh, I can keep a secret," Midge said airily. "I know what he's getting you."

I must have looked dumfounded. I certainly felt that way.

Midge went on, "I was down at Wentworth's Department Store last week and he was in there buying a—well, something. It couldn't'a been for his mother and he hasn't got any sisters. So I knew it was for you. And, boy, was it ever keen!"

"If you dare tell me what it was, Midge Heydon," I threatened, "I'll pin your ears back! I like to be surprised, too."

Midge wrapped her arms around her knees in their grubby blue jeans and grinned up at me teasingly. "I wouldn't tell you for anything," she said, " 'specially since

Brose bought me a double choc'late marshmallow nut sundae so I wouldn't.''

"That's blackmail," I accused, "pure and simple."

"No, it isn't," Midge argued. "I didn't ask him for the sundae, but I wasn't going to turn it down, for creeps' sake. I wouldn't'a told you anyway. I guess I got some principles."

A sort of dreamy look settled over her freckled little face then and she rocked back and forth rhythmically. "I know lots of secrets," she said complacently. "Frinstance, you want'a hear what Adam's Aunt Tess is going to give Alicia and him?"

My mouth dropped open. "How would you know?" I demanded.

Our family's acquaintance with Miss Tess Wentworth is very slight. She lives all alone, except for an old servant, in a great gingerbready house with an iron deer on the lawn. Miss Tess never goes anywhere. Adam and his father, who owns the Wentworth Store, treat her as if she were a queen. And Alicia used to resent their worshipful attitude toward the old lady, but I suppose she has got used to it, now that she's married to Adam. Anyway, so far as I know, the only time Miss Tess had left her house in years was the day of the wedding, when the prospective bride and groom had got so mad at each other it looked as if everything would have to be called off. Midge had taken it upon herself to bring Miss Tess to our house in a taxi to help clear things up, since it was over the grandfather clock Miss Tess had given them that Alicia and Adam had quarreled. But so far as I knew, Midge hadn't laid eyes on her since, any more than I had.

So now I listened in utter amazement as Midge said calmly in answer to my question, "Why, she told me, of course."

"Miss Tess did?"

Midge nodded. "Sure, just yesterday."

"You were there at her house?"

"Why not?" my surprising little sister shrugged. "I go there lots of times."

"And she lets you in?" I demanded.

"She's glad to see me," Midge said. "Kin you blame her? It must get awful' lonesome in that great big house with only Mrs. Fairchild for comp'ny."

"Is Mrs. Fairchild her housekeeper?" I asked.

Midge nodded. "She's not much comp'ny, though. She's awful deaf. But she can sure bake super cookies."

"When did you start going to see Miss Tess?" I had to find out more about this.

"Oh, last summer," Midge recalled, "right after we got home from the lake. I hadn't seen her since the wedding and one day I happened to be going past her house and I thought what a wonderful play horse Blitzen would make, so I tried him out."

"Blitzen?" I repeated.

"Her iron deer," Midge enlightened me. "Only I didn't know what his name was then. And he did make a good horse, except he was sort of hot to sit on, being right out there in the sun. Miss Tess happened to see me—she often sits and looks out through the curtains, just to have something to do. So she had Mrs. Fairchild invite me in for some milk and cookies and we've been good friends ever since."

"Is that so?" I asked rather weakly.

Midge nodded gravely. "I like her a lot," she said. "Sometimes when I'm there we play checkers and sometimes we just sit and talk."

"What in the world about?" I couldn't imagine what they would have in common.

"Oh, lots'a things," Midge said. "She tells me how everything was when she was a little girl and named the deer Blitzen. And I tell her how different it all is now. She hardly ever goes out, you know, so she's sort of behind times. When her relatives go to see her, they just talk about the weather and how well she's looking and unint'resting stuff like that. They don't tell her anything about what's going on in the world. And they all act stiff and dignified. I think Miss Tess enjoys herself more with me."

"I see," I said, smothering my amusement. "Does Mom know you go there?"

Midge considered for a moment, chin on palm. "I don't b'lieve I ever thought to mention it to her. Why, Tobey?" she asked then, solemnly. "You don't think she'd care, do you?"

I shook my head. "I don't see why. She'd probably think it was rather sweet of you, just as I do." I reached out and rumpled her hair affectionately. "You're a queer little bug."

"Why?" Midge's eyes widened in surprise. "I like to go there. Miss Tess has got ever so many strange things in her house. She lets me look around all I like and touch things, too. There's a real suit of armor, like knights used to wear and lots of pretty vases and a picture of Miss Tess when she was eighteen that an artist painted. Only you'd never know it, she's so different now."

I said, "You sound as though you're right at home there."

"I am," Midge admitted. She frowned then. "Only— her house is kind of queer. So gloomy and—quiet. Not a bit like ours."

"No," I agreed drily, "you certainly couldn't call ours gloomy or quiet."

Midge said, after a moment's silence, "She's getting Alicia and Adam a television set for Christmas."

"She is?" I asked, startled. "I didn't suppose she even knew about television."

"She didn't," Midge admitted, "till I told her. Even then she could hardly believe it. She's getting one for herself, too. It'll be lots more int'resting than looking out through the curtains." She wagged her sandy head pityingly. "It must be awful' sad, though, to be so old and all alone on Christmas."

"Alicia and Adam and Mr. Wentworth will be going there Christmas Day," I reminded Midge, feeling a tug of pity at my heart, too.

"It'll be all stiff and stuffy, though," Midge said regretfully. "I think Miss Tess is so old and rich, everybody but me kind of forgets she's human. I know she'd just love all the noise and excitement we have around here on Christmas Eve. I was telling her about it yesterday and she got all sort of chokey and tears came into her eyes. She said it reminded her of Christmases when she was young, with her family all around her. And she said she hoped we all realized how lucky we were—" Midge broke off abruptly and her eyes narrowed as though a startling thought had just occurred to her. She hopped off my bed so fast she knocked the package containing Brose's Argyles to the floor.

"Watch what you're doing," I scolded, retrieving it and straightening the silver ribbon carefully.

But Midge was out in the hall by that time, calling back, "I'm sorry—but I just thought of something. I just thought of something t'rrific! I gotta see Mom about it right away . . ."

Somehow I wasn't very surprised when I went downstairs a little later and found Mom and Midge in a confidential huddle in the kitchen. Mom glanced up as I came in and there was a faintly questioning look in her eye.

She asked me, "What do you think of this idea of Midge's that we invite Adam's aunt over here Christmas Eve? Wouldn't it seem rather queer when we scarcely know her?"

"It wouldn't, Mom," Midge coaxed. "I know her real well."

My mother was still looking questioningly at me, but there was a gentle little smile curving her mouth. "Adam and Alicia will be here, of course. And Mr. Wentworth. But—do you suppose their Aunt Tess would come—or that she'd enjoy herself if she did?"

I said, smiling a little, too, "Midge seems to think so. And I guess she knows her a lot better than you and I do."

"But—we're always so informal Christmas Eve," Mom said doubtfully. "She might find it a little hectic."

"She'd like that," Midge assured us earnestly. "I know she would. Please call her up and ask her, Mom—please!"

Mom spoke in a considering sort of tone, "If the poor old soul is really lonely—"

"She is! I know she is!" Midge was practically popping with excitement. "I'll look up her number for you."

But Mom shook her head. "At least, I'll have to see what your father thinks first."

Dad was just a little bit flabbergasted when he heard about it. But he offered no objection. That's one thing nobody can deny about my parents—they're awfully goodhearted. And neither of them could bear the idea of anyone they knew being lonely or left out of things on Christmas Eve. Secretly, I felt almost as relieved as Midge when they decided definitely to invite Miss Tess to our house. Christmas makes me pretty gushy with sentiment, too.

I think everyone but Midge was surprised, though, when Miss Tess accepted our invitation. Mom said, her voice a little husky as she hung up the receiver after talking with her, "I never would have believed it—but she sounded delighted."

"I told you she would," Midge said smugly.

"I'm so glad we asked her," Mom said then.

And Dad nodded, laying his hand affectionately on Mom's shoulder. "So am I. At least, it'll be a change for her."

"It'll be fun," Midge said positively. "And Miss Tess hardly ever has any fun."

Chapter Nine

A MERRY CHRISTMAS

DICK ALLEN got home from college the next afternoon. My heart skipped a beat as I answered our door bell and saw him standing there in the chill winter sunshine, wearing a warm smile and a belted trench coat, that gave him a movie star air.

He said, "Hi, Tobey," and held my hand tightly in his. "Surprised to see me?"

I shook my head. "The Underground informed me you were expected today." Judy had told Midge, of course, and Midge had told me. I smiled up at Dick as he shut the door behind him. "But I wasn't sure you'd be over so soon."

"Now you're being modest," Dick said.

I was glad I happened to be wearing my gray jersey dress with the wide green snakeskin belt instead of the beat-up jeans and plaid flannel shirt I'd changed from only half an hour earlier. There hadn't been any special reason for getting dressed up, either, except that it was fairly late in the afternoon. Fate must have had a hand in it.

I took Dick into the living room, where a log fire was blazing in the fireplace. Our Christmas tree was already up and trimmed. Mom fights a losing battle every year, trying to restrain the rest of us from setting it up 'way ahead of time. But Dad just can't wait, he's as bad as Midge and I. There was a rich piney odor in the room and sunshine slanted through the west windows. Dick admired the tree and greeted my mother politely when she came in for a minute to say hello. Then we sat down side by side on the couch facing the fire. And—wouldn't you know it?—at that exact moment the doorbell rang again and it was Brose, dropping in without warning!

So all I could do was sit between Dick and Brose on the couch for the next hour or so, trying to keep peace. It's a wonder I didn't simply shrivel with all the baleful glances Brose gave Dick across my defenseless head. But Dick remained suave and poised—and he certainly remained. Of course, nothing short of an earthquake could have jarred Brose loose. Mom came in three times, her hints that it was getting late growing broader and broader, but neither Brose nor Dick seemed to realize what she was getting at.

Finally, when it was quite dark outside and I had had to light the lamps in the living room, my father went along the hall saying in a clear, carrying tone, "I'm starved, Laura. Aren't we ever going to eat?"

That did it. The two boys, eying each other like a pair of belligerent bulldogs, got up and departed—together. At the door Brose said meaningfully, "Be seeing you, Tobey," and Dick said, with no less determination, "I'll be seeing you, too."

I watched them from behind the drapes as they strode down our walk. At the edge of the yard they separated as though they couldn't get away from each other fast enough. I sighed happily and stood there, lost in a lovely dream, till my father's irate voice, calling me to dinner, brought me back to reality with a jerk.

And that was just a sample of how things were going to be all during the holidays. Never have I had a more thrilling whirl. There were moments when I almost suspected Dick and Brose were getting a bigger bang out of thwarting each other than they got out of having a date with me. But, on the whole, it was flattering.

Dick was tied up with his family on Christmas Eve, but Brose, whose folks celebrated Christmas Day, asked me if he couldn't come over for a little while after dinner. So, of course, I said yes, since I knew he was planning to give me my present then and I was naturally curious.

What a dinner we had that night! My father went over to get Miss Tess in our car and Midge went with him. Miss Tess came in on Dad's arm, her wrinkled face all rosy and smiling like a little girl's under her high-riding black velvet hat. Midge was carrying the cutest old-fashioned basket filled with packages that Miss Tess had apparently brought for us all.

"We're so glad you could come," Mom welcomed her.

And Miss Tess answered, holding Mom's hand close in both of her thin blue-veined ones, "Thank you for having me. Midge has told me so much about your wonderful Christmases."

"I hope you won't find it too—hectic," Mom smiled.

"Nonsense!" Miss Tess said, a frosty twinkle in her eye. "Even at my age a wholly calm and settled Christmas seems most dull. That's why I'm everlastingly grateful to you for rescuing me."

Mom sounded a bit choked up, answering her. I was feeling a little chokey, too. It does your heart good to see anyone having as much genuine pleasure as Miss Tess got out of that evening. By the time Alicia and Adam and Mr. Wentworth arrived, she was ensconced on the couch before the fireplace, as much at home as the rest of us.

I could see that the Wentworths were a little startled at their aunt's warmly informal manner. Alicia had told us how Adam and his father always deferred to the old lady and how she responded by being dictatorial and hard to please. But there was certainly nothing of the dragon about Miss Tess that night. So I guess maybe Midge was right about her being grateful for an opportunity to unbend and be treated like a human being instead of a queen.

Dinner was delicious and everyone was very gay. Alicia confided to me in the kitchen as we were helping carry out dishes, "I simply can't get over it! She never acts this way in her own house. You'd think she was a different person entirely."

"Maybe she is," I whispered back. "Wouldn't it warp your personality to be shut up in that old gloomy house, with people making formal calls, bowing and kowtowing to you? I think she's cute."

"Cute?" Alicia sounded slightly strangled. "She used to scare me to death before Adam and I were married." A little smile played around her mouth. "It's certainly a relief to know she has her human side, too."

"See that you remember it," I suggested. "Maybe you'll get along better with her if you do."

After dinner we all adjourned to the living room, where Midge passed out the presents that were stacked like a miniature mountain under the tree. Miss Tess had brought a gift for each of us and tears actually came into her eyes as she opened the presents we had got for her. The linen guest towel Midge had embroidered so painstakingly seemed to touch her most deeply of all, full of bumps and knots though it was.

Afterward, we all gathered around the piano and sang Christmas songs, which Miss Tess played with her stiff old fingers. It was the same sort of Christmas Eve we always had, full of fun and laughter. But you could see it was something special to Miss Tess, something she'd probably cherish in her mind and look back on for months to come. I kept thinking how dreadful it would have been if we hadn't included her. And we wouldn't have thought of it if it hadn't been for Midge. I patted my little sister's shoulder affectionately.

Brose dropped in around eight-thirty and joined in the festivities. I knew he would want to wait till we were alone to give me my present. So I waited with his, too. Mr. Wentworth took Miss Tess home a little before ten, when she began to get tired. She thanked us and told us over and over what a wonderful time she had had. But having her had certainly enriched our Christmas, too, so we thanked her for coming.

Brose and I managed to drift away from the others after that. We sat on the bottom step of the hall stairs, one of our very favorite spots. Mom had got Midge off to bed by that time, so there were just her and Dad and Alicia and Adam left in the living room. We could hear their voices sort of vaguely in the background, but not loud enough to be obtrusive.

Brose said, sticking his chin out a little, "I don't really know whether to give you this or not, the way you've been carrying on with that Allen guy lately." But he slipped a little package out of his jacket pocket just the same.

I set my jaw, too. "You certainly don't have to give me anything you don't want to. And I haven't been carrying on. Just because another man pays a little attention to me—"

"Attention!" Brose interrupted. "He practically lives here. Every time I come over, he's underfoot. I never get you to myself any more." He sounded so woebegone, he

68

almost had me feeling sorry for him. But I steeled myself.

"You have me alone now," I reminded him. "And what do you do? You scold me and argue, even though it's Christmas."

"Aw, Tobey," Brose said softly, reaching out for my hand, "don't let's scrap."

"Well, you started it," I reminded him. But I didn't take my hand away. It felt nice and cozy snuggled in his. I didn't really want to quarrel, either.

"Yeah, I guess I did," Brose admitted. "I'm sorry. But that guy—"

"Let's leave Dick out of it, shall we?" I suggested. I had to use both hands then to reach down to the stair beside me and pick up the two presents I had wrapped for Brose with such loving care. "Merry Christmas," I said softly handing them to him.

"Gee, thanks," Brose said. He balanced the boxes on his knees while he handed me the intriguing little package he had taken from his pocket. "Merry Christmas to you, too."

I thanked him and said, "Open yours first."

"No, you," Brose argued.

But I shook my head. "Please?"

"Well, okay." Manlike, he yanked the elegant silver ribbon off without a qualm. First he opened the box that held the dagger tie-clip I had bought for him. He thought it was perfectly beautiful and proceeded to put it on right away. But when he saw the Argyle socks he was really impressed.

"You didn't knit them yourself?" His tone was sort of hushed, as he stared from them to me unbelievingly.

"Well, practically," I admitted. "Mom helped me a little."

"Gee, Tobey, I sure appreciate them. All that work—gee!"

"You like the colors all right?"

"Yeah, they're swell," Brose said, running his fingers over the socks appreciatively, "just swell. Whenever I wear 'em I'll think of you and all those little stitches you

69

took—" he broke off then to frown at me. "You didn't knit socks for him, too, did you?"

I shook my head. "Those are the only Argyles I ever knit in my whole entire life—and probably the only ones I ever will."

Brose looked relieved. I guess he figured that gave him some sort of advantage over Dick. He said, "Open your present now."

I had been unobtrusively sort of pinching and rattling the little box, but I hadn't yet been able to decide what it was. So now I proceeded to open it and my eyes widened in sheer enchantment as I saw the most beautiful silver compact, shaped like a little envelope and with a lovely long matching lipstick.

"Oh, Brose," I breathed, "it's beautiful."

"Look inside the compact," Brose said, beaming.

So I did and it was engraved, "To Tobey from Brose" and the date. I told him, "It's simply the most wonderful gift I ever got—truly."

"I'd have had 'with love' engraved in it, too," Brose said, "but it costs extra for every letter. And besides that'd have made it seem a little crowded. But I meant 'with love.' You know that, don't you, Tobey?"

I leaned just a little nearer and Brose's arm went around me and he gave me a nice kiss. My heart beat so fast I felt all light-headed. And—wouldn't you know it?—at that exact moment my sister Alicia came out of the living room into the hall and stood there staring at us.

We scrambled apart fast and Brose blushed a rich rose color and my face felt hot, too. I sat waiting miserably for Alicia to make some low sisterly crack, the way she always used to do whenever the opportunity arose. But, as I suspected when I saw her up at college, marriage has definitely had a mellowing influence on my sister. She isn't nearly as big a stinker as she used to be.

She merely smiled at us tolerantly and said, as Adam and my parents came up beside her, "We're all going out to the kitchen to make eggnogs. Don't you two want to come along?"

"Sure, join the party, chillun," Adam grinned.

So we did. And the eggnogs were very good and we all sat around the kitchen drinking them and talking and laughing. And it was one of the very nicest Christmas Eves I can ever remember our having.

Christmas Day was wonderful, too. Dick brought me a big box of candy in the afternoon. Barbie Walters was over at our house with Sox Trevor, when Dick came. So the four of us played records for a while and then went for a walk through the light snow that had begun to fall.

It was lucky Brose was tied up with his family, or the whole afternoon would probably have developed into a situation. As it was, Dick and Barbie and Sox stayed at our house for an informal supper of hot chocolate and cold turkey sandwiches and cookies in front of the fire. And that was no skin off Brose's nose that I could see. But the thought of his reaction if he knew about it made little shivers chase themselves up and down my spine. And I even felt just a little guilty when I powdered my nose with the puff from the lovely engraved compact he had given me.

Still, as my father had insisted so firmly, Brose and I weren't going steady . . .

Chapter Ten

AND A HAPPY NEW YEAR

I suppose it was too much to hope that I'd be able to get through the holidays without Brose really hitting the ceiling over Dick's hanging around. As for Dick, I was a little surprised myself at the rush he was giving me. The memory of Kay Delafield still rankled in my memory. But, I supposed, Dick was spending his time with me because I happened to be available and she wasn't. When he went back to college, that would be the end of it.

But Brose wasn't inclined to be so tolerant. A couple

of days before New Year's he called up and asked if he could come over.

"Why, of course," I told him. "Come ahead."

"I want to talk to you," he said meaningfully, "alone. Will you go for a walk—a long walk?"

"I'd love to," I said, with more conviction than I actually felt. It wasn't that I didn't like to walk with Brose. But I could tell by his tone he was going to be difficult.

And I was so right!

I wore slacks and a warm jacket and my earmuffs and mittens and sheepskin-lined boots. Brose was dressed for the cold, too. We hiked out along Lake Road, between banks of snow piled up by the big snowplow. You could hear the snow crunching underfoot and the sky was so blue and the sunshine so bright you almost needed dark glasses. Our breath clouded before us and Brose's mittened hand held mine tight as we walked along. That was a good sign, at least.

I had a pretty good idea where we were heading. Out a little beyond the lake, there's a farmer's fence that sticks up above the snow. Brose and I have had several of our most serious conversations perched on its top rail. It was there that I agreed to wear his class ring and it was also there that he put the ring on my finger for the first time. I felt a sort of sinking sensation in my tummy as we went floundering through the snowbanks toward the familiar rail fence. Exactly what had Brose brought me away out here to say to me?

He didn't keep me in suspense very long. As he boosted me up onto the top rail and sat down beside me he said, "All right now. There are some things we gotta get straightened out between us. A fella's got a right to know where he stands."

I told him, "You stand just where you always have with me, Brose. Why do you talk as if everything's different?"

"What about Allen?" Brose demanded.

"Dick's—just a good friend," I said.

"Yeah, but you're wearing *my* class ring," Brose argued.

"Maybe," I said, very low and sort of hesitantly, "you'd rather I gave it back. Any time you feel that way—"

"I don't, though," Brose said miserably. "You know I don't, Tobey. You know how I feel about you. But that guy's been in my hair ever since he got home last week. He's taken you to the movies and skating, he hangs around your house all the time."

I said reasonably, "Brose, listen to me. You know I've told you all along my parents said we were absolutely not to figure we were going steady. If I act as though we are, they'll object right away, they won't want me to keep your ring."

"Yeah, I suppose so," Brose sounded glum. "And it was okay before he got home. The guys at school know a class ring means 'keep off'—I don't see why he's so dumb."

"He's not dumb," I had to defend Dick. "Maybe it's just that—when you get older, as Dick is, you look at things like class rings and all that—well, differently."

"He's not so old," Brose argued. "Nineteen's all. And I'm going to be eighteen before long myself."

"I know," I said. "I didn't mean you were young."

"Why doesn't he get himself a girl his own age?" Brose demanded. "Somebody up at college—"

"Maybe he has," I suggested. "Maybe he's just being nice to me because I'm handy at the moment."

"Very unlikely," Brose growled. "He asked you up to college for that dance, didn't he?"

"Well—yes, but—" I let it go at that.

Brose shook his head. "He's got a crush on you—a bad one. I ought'a push his face in."

"Don't be ridiculous!" I said. But I couldn't help feeling a delicious little thrill at the thought of Brose and Dick actually coming to blows—over me! Not that I wanted them to, really, not that I wouldn't do everything I could to stop them—still the thought was exciting. I guess there's a teeny trace of the cave woman left in us, no matter how civilized we imagine ourselves.

Brose said darkly, "Yeah, that's exactly what I ought'a do."

"Brose Gilman, if you dared—" I said faintly.

"You think I couldn't lick him?" Brose demanded.

I certainly wasn't going to enter into a discussion of who would lick whom. From where I sat, it looked as though it might be pretty much of a toss-up—both Dick and Brose were very big and male.

I said firmly, "If you don't stop acting so—so infantile, I will give your ring back. I'll give it back right now—" I pulled my hand out of Brose's, as though I were going to suit action to the word that minute.

Brose grabbed my hand again quickly. He looked a little scared, so I guessed I'd sounded convincing enough. He begged, "Tobey, don't. I want you to wear it—only, gee whiz—"

"Look, Brose." I let my hand relax in his. It was hard not to feel sorry for him when he sounded so completely miserable. "Let's just be reasonable about the whole thing, shall we? Let's discuss alternatives calmly and not go blowing our tops. You don't want me to give your ring back—right?"

Brose nodded positively. "That's right."

"And my parents say we're not to go steady, so I can't very well refuse to have anything to do with other men."

"Well—yeah—but—"

I let a little smile curve my mouth as I looked up at him. "Doesn't it seem to you we're sort of making a big thing out of nothing? I mean, in just a few more days Dick'll be back at college and everything will be the way it was before."

"Yeah," Brose said, brightening a little, "I guess that's true enough."

"Of course, it's true," I pressed my advantage. "So if you'll just be reasonable—"

"But what about spring vacation?" Brose broke in. "He'll be home then, too—and all summer long, I suppose."

"By then he may not be interested in me at all," I said. But I couldn't help feeling a small forlorn qualm at the possibility. "Or you and I may have broken up." That gave me a qualm, too.

"What are you talking about?" Brose demanded gruffly. "We won't do anything of the sort!"

"Well—I don't know," I said, "if you're going to be so unreasonable and demanding all the time."

"I won't," Brose said earnestly. "I'll try to make the best of things while he's here, if only you won't talk about us breaking up. I mean—well, gosh, Tobey, you know how I feel about you."

I gave his hand a little hard squeeze and jumped down off the fence. "I feel the same way, Brose. But now we'd better be getting back before we turn into a couple of icicles sitting out here in this wind. Race you to the road. Last one there's a monkey's uncle."

As we went floundering off through the snowdrifts like a herd of turtles, I couldn't help feeling I'd handled that ticklish situation rather well . . .

The last half of the holidays was just as much fun as the first half had been. Or maybe a little more, since Brose tried to be a bit more reasonable about my dates with Dick. I went with Brose to Barbie Walters' skating party and with Dick to Kay Lamb's sleigh ride. Brose too Mary Andrews, of all people, on the sleigh ride. I felt a little burned-up about that at first. But then my sense of fair play prodded me out of it. I guess if I could date Dick, Brose could date Mary—although what he can see in her is simply beyond me. But I guess there is just no accounting for men's taste.

Sox Trevor, whose house has a lovely big rumpus room in the basement, with a fireplace and soft drink bar, threw a perfectly marvelous New Year's party for the whole crowd. The girls all decided beforehand to wear long dresses, although the boys spurned the mere idea of tuxedos at a private party in someone's house. Men are so funny about getting dressed up. I know my mother always has a dreadful time getting my father into his dinner jacket, so I guess such reluctance is just a natural attribute of the male sex.

Brose took me to Sox's party and Dick took Kay Lamb. I wondered if he had been moved to ask her partly because she had the same first name as his girl up at college, Kay Delafield. But I guess that was just a sort of catty thought on my part and maybe Dick liked Kay for herself alone, which wouldn't be too difficult as she is quite an attractive girl with a warm vivacious personality and one of my best friends. Anyway, he had asked me to the party first, not knowing I had already promised to go with Brose. So there was really no sting in seeing Dick with Kay. And he danced with me quite a bit anyway—enough to arouse Brose's jealous resentment.

I had a wonderful time at the party. Sox has a terrific collection of records and we danced to most of them. Also we played games and ate the wonderful food Mrs. Trevor had prepared for us—stacks of sandwiches and great bowls of potato chips and two or three different kinds of cake and gallons of soft drinks. At midnight we blew horns and broke balloons and sang "Auld Lang Syne" in a big circle with our arms locked together. Everybody was kissing and laughing and wishing everyone else "Happy New Year."

Dick caught my eye from across the room and lifted his glass to his lips in a silent meaningful toast. Brose saw what he was doing and scowled ferociously. I couldn't remember a New Year's Eve that had been more fun.

Then we all got to wondering aloud where we'd be next New Year. And then we got to talking about where we'd been last year at this same time. It turned out that most of us had been at a big party at my house. But not Dick. The Allens hadn't even lived in Edgewood then. I hadn't known Dick last New Year. It hardly seemed possible when we were such good friends now.

A little later, when I happened to be dancing with him, he confided to me that the very same thought had struck him. "I guess time hasn't too much to do with friendship," he said. "When you meet someone you really like, it seems as if you know them well, anyway."

I had to admit that this was true. Dick's cheek pressed lightly against my hair as we danced. He was a marvelous dancer—as good as Brose, if not a teensy bit better. Our steps matched, so I never had to think about my feet at all. Of course, I didn't have to think about my feet when I danced with Brose, either—but we'd been dancing together for years.

Dick said, "We won't be seeing each other for a while, Tobey. I have too much cramming to do to get home very often. I might not get back more than once before spring vacation."

"That's months off," I said, feeling sad at the thought.

"Yeah," Dick sounded as unhappy as I felt. "Suppose you might squeeze in time to write me once in a while?"

"You write and I'll answer," I agreed. This was a fairly safe thing to say, since it has been my experience that most men are very procrastinating when it comes to writing letters. Lots of women are, too, including me.

Dick asked softly, his lips close to my ear, "Will you miss me a little?"

I nodded. "Will you miss me?"

"Too much," Dick said.

I couldn't resist the temptation to ask, "Even with Kay Delafield right there all the time?"

After a silent moment Dick said, "I had a hunch you'd heard something about Kay when you were up at Central. But you didn't say anything at the time—and I wasn't sure."

I shrugged. "What was there to say? A girl can't always be first choice, I suppose."

Dick said huskily, holding me just a little closer as we danced, "I hope you weren't hurt or—or unhappy about it, Tobey. I hope it didn't spoil things for you. The thing was, when Kay stood me up I was pretty desperate. I cast around in my mind for some girl who was a knockout, who'd show Kay she wasn't so terrific."

So it had been the way Geri Clair had suspected. I even felt flattered now, hearing Dick go on, "So I thought of you. At first, my main idea was to use you to put Kay in her place. But when you were up at school and we had such a swell time—well, to tell you the absolute truth, I haven't given Kay much thought since."

"Haven't you really, Dick?" My heart fluttered against my ribs like a captive butterfly.

He shook his head. "So help me," he said. "None of the girls up at school have made much of an impression on me. I keep comparing them with you."

"You're just saying that." Even if it was a line, I loved it.

But Dick argued, "Why else do you suppose I looked you up as soon as I got home? Why do you think I've been camping on your doorstep ever since, getting your local boy all riled up, risking life and limb—" Dick broke off to whisper, "Here he comes now, looking mad enough to break me in two with his bare hands. Only I can't blame the poor guy. I'd feel the same way in his place."

Brose's look said quite plainly to Dick, "Drop dead!" But aloud he said, with elaborate politeness, "Mind if I cut in?"

Dick's look was very superior and man-of-the-world and, I knew, utterly infuriating to Brose, as he relinquished me with a murmured, "Not at all." There wasn't much else Dick could do. Brose was my date. And Kay Lamb was Dick's. And Dick and I had been dancing together through two or three records, which surely was the equivalent of one regular dance.

Brose growled savagely into my ear, as we danced away from Dick, "I ought'a push his face in!"

"Why?" I asked innocently. "Because he danced with me? You ought to push Sox's face in, too, then—and all the rest of the boys."

"You don't look like you're enjoying it so much when you dance with the others," Brose said darkly.

"That's just your imagination," I said.

But I could tell by his expression that I hadn't convinced him.

"All I hope," Brose said between clenched teeth, "is that I can hold out till he goes back to college."

Chapter Eleven

AN EMERGENCY ARISES

SOMETHING happened right after New Year's that gave us all quite a jolt. We were sitting around the living room one night, pretty much as usual. Mom was thumbing through a new magazine, Dad was reading the evening paper. Midge had her head in the radio, listening to some horse opera and I was doing my nails and sort of thinking back over the lovely two weeks just past. School seemed even duller than usual after all the excitement. And I missed Dick rather more than I had expected to. Or maybe it was just the fun of having two men interested in me that I missed. Now if the phone rang, and a male voice asked for me, it would be Brose. There wouldn't be any element of uncertainty involved. But it wasn't that I was any less fond of Brose than before—it was just—

Well, I asked myself somewhat severely, what was it exactly? Was I simply one of those fickle women who can't make up their minds about what man they want and so try to hang onto every male in sight? But I really wasn't like that. Look at all the men I knew that I never felt the slightest yen for, Sox and Itchy and the rest. None of my girl friends had ever accused me of being a grabber, like Mary Andrews. None of them ever worried about their favorite men dancing with me, or pairing off for tennis or badminton doubles. Well, then! It must simply be that I liked Dick quite a bit. Of course, I liked Brose a lot, too. That's what had made it so thrilling and flattering, having them both around to give me a rush.

My thoughts were milling pleasantly like that, not really

getting anywhere, but enjoying the trip, when the phone rang.

"I'll get it," I said and ambled out into the hall, expecting it to be Brose, or maybe Barbie Walters.

But it was Western Union saying they had a wire for Mrs. Henry Heydon. My heart started beating fast as I called Mom. There's something so unsettling about wires. Maybe, I thought, as Mom hurried to take the phone from me, this would be some word from Janet. Maybe the baby had come earlier than the fifteenth, when it was expected. Maybe we'd know now whether it was a boy or girl.

Dad had followed Mom out into the hall and he and I hovered around as she listened intently to the message. We tried to read something from her expression and when I saw the frown between her eyes getting deeper, my throat choked up. Could it be bad news—something wrong? Was Janet—?

"Yes," Mom said into the phone, "I got it all plainly. Thank you."

She hung up and swung around excitedly to face us. "It was from Janet," she told us. "Henry, you must wire her right back and tell her I'm coming. If I get the morning train to Chicago, I can catch a night plane for California."

"Now wait a minute," Dad said, looking pale suddenly. "Is it Janet—or the baby—what on earth—?"

Mom squeezed his hand reassuringly. "Nothing's wrong with Janet or the baby. It hasn't been born yet."

"Toots then?" Dad gulped. "Or is it Jim?"

"No, no," Mom shook her head. "They're all fine—or at least the wire didn't imply there was anything the matter with any of them."

"Then what," my father demanded irately, his face getting quite red by contrast with its previous paleness, "is all this nonsense about you getting trains and planes?"

"Now, Henry," Mom soothed, "if you'll just let me explain, you'll see I have no alternative. It's the woman Janet was going to have to stay with little Jimmy while she's in the hospital. She's broken her leg and she'll be in a cast for weeks and the baby's due in ten days and naturally Janet's frantic, she has no idea of anyone else she could get, so she wired me. And if I take a plane tomorrow night I can be there Friday. So you wire Janet and tell her that, while I pack."

"Well—okay," Dad said. "Only why didn't you say so in the first place instead of scaring me half to death?"

Isn't it wonderful to have such parents? Even away out there in California, Janet had known she could depend on them. All she had to do was let them know she was in a jam and here was Mom, halfway up the stairs already on her way to pack and Dad, hunting around for a pencil to compose a wire to send Janet. My heart swelled with loving pride in them. You couldn't ever let people like that down, any more than they'd let you down.

Suddenly Mom turned on the stairs and stood there, her hand gripping the banister, a stricken look on her face. "Oh my goodness!" she exclaimed.

"Now what?" Dad looked up from scribbling on the back of an old envelope.

I looked up at her, too, rather blankly. It was on my face that Mom's troubled glance was fixed.

"I was so worried over Janet's predicament," Mom told me, "I forgot all about you—and poor little Midge."

"There's nothing wrong with Midge and me," I said, still not getting it.

"No, of course not," Mom said. "But—what'll you do? How will you get along without me here?"

"Well—we'll miss you," I admitted. "But we can certainly get along for a few weeks. After all, I'm seventeen and Midge—"

"She's just a baby," Mom said in a sort of brooding tone. "And you have no more idea of keeping house than —than your father."

"Now just a minute," Dad said. "I'll have you know you're insulting our intelligence, both mine *and* Tobey's. And Midge is far from being a baby."

"A *baby!*" Midge exclaimed in an utterly revolted tone

from the living room doorway behind us. "Who says I'm a baby?"

Apparently she was through listening to her night's stint of riding and rescuing and had wandered out to the hall just in time to get in on the tail end of our conversation. So nothing would do but she must have a full explanation.

And when it had been given her, she said staunchly to Mom, "What you worrying about us for? We'll be all right. Daddy can take care of us."

"But you'll be at work," Mom addressed Dad worriedly. "You might even have to go out of town."

Dad's job as salesman for a plumbing supply company does mean he has to travel sometimes. But he said now, "I'll see to it that I don't. And anyway, Tobey's grown up."

Isn't it funny, the way a parent's viewpoint changes, depending on circumstances? Sometimes Dad makes me sound as if I'm about twelve years old and not too bright. Now you'd think I was a woman of twenty-five at the very least.

Mom sighed and sort of wrung her hands. "Oh, dear," she said, "I do hope you'll be able to manage. I just don't see how I can let Janet down. She shouldn't have a lot of worry on her mind at a time like this—and poor little Jimmy—"

I said, "We'll get along perfectly okay, you'll see. After all, Midge and I will both be at school all day. And Dad will be here nights. What could possibly happen?"

"Women," Dad said, "always try to make it seem as if taking care of a house and family is a job no mere male is competent to tackle. When, as a matter of fact, men have figured out more efficient systems for organizing housework on a business-like basis, saving time and steps, than any woman ever did. All your efficiency experts, with very few exceptions, are men. And it's a known fact—"

"Oh, dear," Mom sighed again, starting up the stairs slowly. She spoke to me across her shoulder. "Why don't you come up with me now and I'll tell you everything you'll have to do."

"Mom, for heaven's sake," I said, a trifle miffed at her utter lack of confidence in my ability and common sense, "I guess I know how to keep house. Anyone can do that. There's nothing complicated about it. If you'll just lay down the law to Midge, so she'll know she has to mind me—"

"I know how to act," Midge said aggrievedly, "without you bossing me around. And I can make my own bed and keep my room tidier than you do yours."

"Is that so?" I began.

But Dad said sternly, "Now listen here, you two. Don't start quarreling at a time like this. Can't you see your mother has enough on her mind?"

"I'm sorry." I smiled up at Mom reassuringly. "I'll come help you pack. And don't you go worrying the teeniest bit about how we'll get along. You just take care of things for Janet till she gets back on her feet and we'll manage. We'll manage perfectly well."

I looked at Dad and Midge for corroboration and they nodded solemnly. But Mom didn't seem too relieved . . .

She took the ten o'clock train for Chicago the next morning. It being a school day, I had to say good-bye to her before I left at eight-fifteen. By that time she had given me such a complete briefing, I felt as if I'd be quite capable of managing a twenty-room house and a family three times the size of ours. I couldn't think of one little detail of home management Mom had neglected to enlighten me on. And, apparently, neither could she.

She let me leave for school at last with an earnest, "Now you don't think you'll have any trouble, do you, dear?"

I assured her for probably the fiftieth time that I wouldn't. "Don't you worry now. We'll be fine."

"I hope so." Mom smiled wanly and gave me a tight hug and a big kiss. "And I'll be back just as soon as Janet's able to cope with things, I promise."

We said good-bye then and I had to run practically all the way to school.

Brose found the idea of my keeping house very funny. I told him about it that afternoon as we were walking home and he looked sort of startled for a minute and then burst into a loud laugh. "Not you, Tobey," he managed to get out between bellows of mirth. "I never thought of you as the domestic type."

"I'm so glad it doesn't show," I said a trifle tartly. Honestly, the way everyone was taking this, you'd think I was a nitwit or something.

"Look," Brose demanded unbelievingly, "you mean you're actually going to pinch-hit for your mother? You mean you're going to cook, too?"

"Anyone can cook if they can read," I informed him. "There are cookbooks, you know."

"Do they tell how to boil water?" Brose asked waggishly.

I glared at him. "I can cook lots of things without even looking at a cookbook."

"For instance?"

"Well—hamburgers and—eggs." I thought a second. "And fudge."

"Doesn't sound like a very balanced diet," Brose shook his head.

"Well, you don't have to eat my cooking," I informed him. "So don't worry."

"Look," Brose said, grinning, "I'll tell you what I'll do. I'll buy you a hamburger and a malted at Joe's right now, so you won't have to worry about your own dinner anyway."

"Thank you so much," I said bitingly, "but no." I felt a small qualm then. "Can't stop at Joe's after school while Mom's away," I informed him. "Mom doesn't want Midge left on the loose, so I have to go straight home from school."

"Gee," Brose said sympathetically, "that's tough."

"Besides," I explained, "at first it may take me quite a while to get dinner, just till I get used to it, that is. So I really should go straight home anyway."

"Yeah, I suppose so," Brose said glumly. He asked then,

"Can I come over for a while tonight, though? I thought maybe you wouldn't mind helping me with my French a little."

"I shouldn't," I said darkly, "after all that razzing about my cooking and my ability to keep house."

"Aw, Tobey," Brose said earnestly, "you know I didn't mean it."

So I weakened and said he could come over at eight. I figured that would give me ample time to get all the work out of the way.

Chapter Twelve

I TAKE OVER

THE HOUSE seemed sort of chill and empty when I went in. Everything was clean and in order. Naturally Mom would have left it that way. But I couldn't help realizing what a difference her being gone made. It was as if the house didn't have any heart without her. But that was just imagination on my part, I told myself. If she'd been at Woman's Club, or playing bridge somewhere, I wouldn't have given it a thought. But just because I knew she was on her way to California, I was being silly.

Midge came in then, with Judy Allen and another little friend in tow, and bedlam broke loose. I was secretly glad.

Midge yelled, "Hi, Tobey. We're gonna play horses."

And Judy yelled, "I wanna have a snow fight. It's keen packing. Let's, Midge."

But Midge was adamant and the other little girl backed her up, so Judy was outnumbered.

I said, sounding just like Mom, "Take off those snowy boots before you drip all over everything. And you'll have to pick up your horses when you finish playing."

I left them struggling out of their wraps in the hall

and wandered out to the kitchen. There was a note from Mom propped on the table.

It read: "Cookbook and recipe file in second cabinet left sink. Lots of things in freezer. Needn't shop for food till Saturday. Just remember everything I told you and you shouldn't have a bit of trouble. At least, I hope not. Love, Mom."

I smiled a little as I read. Then my smile faded. Just what had Mom told me? So many, many things. And I'd been so excited about her leaving and about Janet's problems, I hadn't paid too much attention. Let's see now, I thought back. Mrs. Blue was going to do the laundry. Mom had said if I gave the house one good cleaning a week and a couple of light goings-over, it should suffice. There had been something about defrosting the refrigerator, but I thought that only had to be done once a week. And I must be sure to keep the buttons sewed on Dad's shirts. That was practically the only thing he was fussy about. And there had been something about the egg man —what day did he come? And Mom had said Dad would be sure to take care of paying the bills, only I might have to remind him. I began to feel a little confused, as I tried to track down all the vital instructions Mom had given me. Maybe there was a tiny bit more to this job of running a house than I had imagined.

Right now, though, there was dinner. First things first, I thought virtuously. I got out one of Mom's aprons and tied it around me. I rolled up my sleeves. It was only four o'clock and Dad never got home much before six. Still, just this first night, I'd be on the safe side and allow myself plenty of time. Later on, I'd be able to start dinner at five, the way Mom usually did. Getting a meal together always seemed so easy for her. And it was easy, I assured myself staunchly as I headed for the second cabinet left of the sink, where Mom had said she kept her cookbook . . .

It was a good thing I'd told Brose not to come over till eight. Honestly, the trouble I had with that dinner you wouldn't believe! The chops were all done and shriveling before the potatoes had hardly begun to bake. They seemed to take forever. Besides, I forgot to salt the peas and the salad had too much vinegar in it. And why I decided on Brown Betty for dessert, I'll never know. It turned out burned on top and raw in the middle. The whole dinner was a mess.

Midge set the table for me of her own accord. But even so, I was pretty near tears by the time Dad got home. I had burned my wrist and cut my hand with the can opener.

"Now just you take it easy, baby," Dad said solicitously. "I'll have everything on the table in no time."

It took him considerably longer than that. And he burned his hand, too, and spilled a lot of peas on the floor and used some quite strong language. But eventually everything was as ready as it would ever be, so we sat down and tried to eat it.

Midge said, "Phooey!" after one taste of her salad.

"Now, Midge, that's not the proper spirit," Dad reproached her. "Tobey's doing the best she can."

But I noticed he wasn't eating much, either. I couldn't really blame him. Everything tasted horrible.

"How long will Mom be gone?" Midge asked in a brave resigned tone out of a lengthy silence in which all anyone did was chew.

"It depends," Dad told her, "on when the baby arrives."

"I hope it comes soon," Midge said, pushing her peas around on her plate.

I gave her a mean look. "You act as though it's a perfectly simple thing to just start in being an expert cook without any practice."

"You help Mom sometimes," Midge pointed out.

"That's different," I said hotly. And it was. With Mom there to tell me just what to do, it was easy. I added lamely, "I'll do better when I get used to it."

"Of course you will," Dad said soothingly. "This wasn't—" he sort of gulped, "bad at all for an initial effort."

He is really very sweet. I gave him a tender smile.

He went on, "The thing is, we need some sort of system around here. I've always felt system is just as important in running a home as any other business. But your mother—well, she never would take me seriously."

I asked reasonably, because certainly I hadn't distinguished myself by the method I'd started out with, "What sort of a system?"

"Well," Dad said, "I'd have to put some thought on it, of course."

Midge asked, "Couldn't Tobey just read in the cookbook how to make stuff?"

I glared at her. "I did read the cookbook! But they—well, they just seem to take it for granted that you know how long some things take to cook."

"Don't they say how much vinegar to put in the salad?"

"My hand sort of slipped," I had to admit.

"Cooking," Dad said portentously, "is just a matter of practice, anyway. Tobey will get onto that."

"I hope so," Midge said, looking sort of sick. I saw that she'd just swallowed a big bite of her Brown Betty.

"But system," Dad went on, "is important. With system a person can run a house more efficiently and with much less effort."

I pricked up my ears.

Dad shoved his half-eaten dessert aside and a horrible thought struck me. I had absolutely forgotten to make coffee. And anyone who has lived in the same house with my father for seventeen years knows how he loves his coffee.

"Never mind," Dad said in a rather pained tone when I confessed. "I guess I drink too much anyway."

"I'll be glad to put some on to perk now," I told him.

But Dad shook his head. "We were discussing a system of doing housework. I was reading an article only the other day where it told how they had counted the number of steps it took the average woman while she was preparing a meal, making a bed, cleaning house and so on. Then it showed how all that footwork could be cut in half or more, just by using a proper system. For instance, all the pans should be kept close to the stove instead of being put away inconveniently in cabinets."

"Wouldn't that be a little untidy?" I asked doubtfully.

"There you go," Dad said, "being female, just like your mother. That's exactly what she said when I told her how many hundreds of steps she could save every day. I think women like to make martyrs of themselves."

"Not me," I argued. "The less work, the better, so far as cooking and keeping house are concerned—that's the way I feel."

"You do?" Dad asked, a sort of awe-struck expression settling over his face. "You mean you'd try out a system if I work one out for you?"

I nodded. What did I have to lose?

"That's wonderful!" Dad said. "That's great, Tobey!" He pushed back his chair. "I guess it's just a question of finding a woman young enough to have a receptive mind instead of being firmly set in her ways, bent and determined to do things the way women have always done them." He laid a firmly approving hand on my shoulder. "I'll get at it right away, tonight. I'll figure out every detail. Who knows, maybe I'll go down in history as the man who emancipated the female sex from their drudgery, broke the bonds that shackled them to their uninspiring treadmill of backbreaking labor."

"I thought it was Edison was supposed to do that when he invented 'lectricity," Midge put in. "We read it in our history book."

"That," Dad said grandly, "was only the beginning, my child."

I glanced at my watch and got hastily to my feet. In less than an hour Brose would be coming over and I looked like an absolute witch. Then a shattering realization struck me.

I told Midge, "You've got to help with the dishes and clearing the table and all."

She said, affronted, "But I set it for you!"

"Well, I got dinner for you," I pointed out. Then, at her look, I added, "Even if you didn't like it."

Dad said firmly, "That's right, Midge. You'll have to consider helping with the dishes one of your regular jobs from now on."

Midge let out a moan like a wounded elephant.

"Come on, get going," I said wearily. "The sooner we start, the sooner we'll be finished."

"Yes, indeed," Dad said, heading for the library. "And while you two take care of that, I'll get started on the System."

Isn't that just like a man?

Chapter Thirteen

I AGREE TO BE A GUINEA PIG

I WAS still upstairs getting myself put together after my struggle with a mountain of dishes and greasy burned pans when Brose came. Midge let him in and I could hear her telling him, "She'll be down in a few minutes—she *says*."

"How was dinner?" Brose asked wickedly.

"Cruddy," Midge said, with customary childish candor.

"Oh, well," Brose said loyally, "she'll learn."

He wandered on into the library then, where I heard a vague murmur of voices as he greeted my father. Fifteen minutes later, when I went downstairs, my hair brushed, my wounds bandaged, my lipstick freshened and my hastily donned plaid wool jumper making me look like a fairly glamorous character instead of a household drudge, I found Dad and Brose, their heads close together, hunched over a big sheet of paper at the desk.

"Hi," I said, when neither of them looked around.

Brose glanced up a shade absently. "Oh, hi, Tobey," he said. Then he addressed my father, "How about the washing and ironing? You got a time figured out for that?"

"What are you talking about?" I demanded. "Mom's got a woman all arranged for to take care of the laundry."

"Oh. Oh, has she?" It seemed to me I could detect a

faint note of regret in my father's voice. "I was just figuring they'd be easy to fit in—"

"What are you two doing?" I managed to get my head in between Dad's and Brose's in order to study the big chart they were so busy with.

"This," Dad said importantly, "is the Henry Heydon Comprehensive Schedule for Efficient Homemaking. I called it that," he explained, "because I understand women today prefer to think of themselves as homemakers rather than housekeepers. And I'll admit there is a—well, a certain degree more dignity in the term. Anyway, this is it. Of course, there are a few more details I have to work out —but what do you think of it?"

I didn't say a word for a minute. I was too intent on the result of Dad's labors. It was a big square, ruled off into seven smaller sections, each headed with a day of the week. Under each day various tasks were listed, worked out according to a sort of timetable. I felt myself paling with horror.

"But I can't carry out anything like this," I gulped. "All the time I'll have will be after school and week-ends."

"We know that," Brose said soothingly. You'd think the Comprehensive Schedule for Efficient Homemaking was his idea. He seemed as enthusiastic about it as Dad was. "Your father is going to work out an Adjusted Version for you, aren't you, Mr. Heydon?"

"Of course," my father said, making a bit of lettering a little plainer. "Also the Adjusted Version will serve for women who have jobs outside their homes and so don't have a full quota of time to devote to their homemaking duties."

"I'm glad you realize that includes me," I said weakly. "I don't suppose Mom would like it if I quit school to carry out your ideas while she's gone."

Dad gave me a reproachful look. I couldn't imagine what had happened to his wonderful sense of humor. He said, "I see no reason to be facetious about this, Tobey. You said you'd be willing to try out my ideas."

I smiled halfheartedly. "Just call me Guinea Pig."

Now Brose was frowning at me, too. "Honestly," he addressed my father, very superior and man-to-man, "if that isn't gratitude for you!"

"Gratitude!" I exclaimed indignantly. "I didn't ask anybody to go to all this trouble. It was Dad's idea."

"It certainly was," Dad admitted with quiet pride. "Why, this System could mean the complete revolutionizing of housework for millions of women all over the country. Instead of a slapdash, do-it-when-the-spirit-moves-you way of carrying out their work, everything will be done in an efficient businesslike manner. For instance, shopping for food, that will all be done at a specified time on a specified day, none of this wasting time running to the store for a loaf of bread or a pound of butter."

"Mom always shops on Fridays," I pointed out. "Of course, she sometimes forgets a thing or two, or maybe runs out of something."

"A perfect example," my father informed Brose, "of feminine thinking. Forgetting, running out of things—the Heydon System does away with all that, puts things on an absolutely businesslike basis."

Brose nodded in profound agreement. "Now my mother," he said, "would certainly profit by something like this. Some weeks she cleans the house two or three times and others only once."

"Maybe," I pointed out scathingly, "it hinges on whether she's having a lot of company, or whether you track in a lot of mud on your big feet."

Brose and my father looked at each other with maddening smiles, as if they were merely tolerating my childish prattle.

"Women," my father said, "always try to make it sound as though housework simply cannot be organized efficiently."

Brose nodded. "I guess that kind of makes them feel important, having some new pee-wee crisis to cope with every other minute."

"Is that so!" I began, glaring at him.

But my father cut in, "Now, Tobey, don't go getting mad. We're only trying to help you. Look at all the trouble you had, just getting dinner tonight. And it's going to be even harder for you to take over full-scale housekeeping."

"I'll manage," I said coldly. But at the stricken look on my father's face, I felt my anger melt a little.

He said, "But, Tobey, you said you'd try out my ideas if I worked out a system. You said so right at the table."

I guessed I had, at that.

"Okay," I sighed. "Only let's keep it somewhere within reason, shall we? Let's not get carried away."

"Of course not," Dad agreed, beaming again. "Reason is at the base of the whole business. You'll see."

He and Brose hunched over their precious chart again.

"I'm going to do my homework," I announced after a couple of minutes of being absolutely ignored. I started toward the living room.

"Be with you in a minute, Tobey," Brose said.

I settled down in front of the smouldering log fire, my books strewn around me. I did my Lit assignment and my Civics. I struggled with my Math, with no help whatever from Brose. I suppose it was because I'd had such an ordeal with dinner and the dishes that I felt so drowsy. The last thing I remembered as I sort of snuggled down for a minute with a pillow from the couch was the vague murmur of masculine voices from the library.

Then Dad was shaking my shoulder and I sat up with a terrific crick in my neck. I yawned widely. "Where's Brose?"

"I sent him home," Dad said. "It's pretty late. You'd better get to bed, Tobey. You've had kind of a hard day."

"But his French," I objected. "I promised to help him."

"Oh, was that why he came over?" Dad asked. "He must have forgotten all about it. We got so involved in the Adjusted Version of the Schedule, the one I worked out for you, that the time sort of got away from us." He smiled at me reassuringly, "But it's all finished, Tobey. I tacked it up on the bulletin board in the kitchen. And

Saturday I'm going to fix up a lot of step-saving devices. You won't have to worry about a thing now. All you need do is follow the Schedule to the letter."

I got up and stretched and yawned again. I wasn't feeling very intelligent at the moment, or I might have put up some argument. Just then it seemed more important that Brose would be in a heck of a fix over not having his French assignment the next day. But that was his hard luck, I reminded myself . . .

As was to be expected, my cooking improved gradually. After all, it couldn't get worse. If I hadn't promised, in a weak moment, to carry out Dad's Comprehensive Schedule, things would probably have run quite smoothly. Instead, my life became more and more complicated. The thing was, Dad took the Schedule so seriously, I didn't have the heart to tell him what I really thought of it. Honestly, it just seems as if men never grow up!

That first Saturday Dad got busy with his tool kit and some lumber he had in the basement and began fixing up a sort of combination shelf and hanging-space for pans. This he set up right next to the stove in order to save steps when getting a meal. Theoretically, it might not have been such a bad idea. But my father, to put it mildly, is no carpenter and the final results of his efforts, besides a smashed thumb and some bad dents in the surrounding woodwork, was a very wobbly-looking affair indeed. I quaked to think what Mom would have to say about it.

Next Dad rearranged all the cabinets and I must admit that, by the time he had finished, it was possible for me to assemble a complete meal with very little footwork. However, it had never been the footwork involved that bothered me, it was the handwork. But I couldn't quite bring myself to dissipate his proud pleasure by telling him so.

Next he devised a sort of kit, containing furniture polish, glass-cleaner, all sorts of cleaning cloths and brushes. This I was supposed to carry around with me, from room to room, as I cleaned the house. Basically, I suppose this was a sound enough idea, too. It was supposed to save me those countless trips back to the kitchen for different things I needed in the course of my work. And it did. But the trouble was, carrying all the stuff with me, in addition to lugging the dust mop and shoving the vacuum cleaner, tired me more than the extra steps would have.

Also my father proceeded to work out a new improved method of making beds, which took only five movements. I practically tied my spinal column in knots trying to carry it out under Dad's critical eye. Of course, when he wasn't around I didn't bother with it. But I had to bribe Midge not to tell on me by letting her store a stock of snowballs in the deep-freeze. She and Judy Allen made them and put them away carefully, with the idea of having a snowball fight next July or August, when it would be a lot more fun than in the middle of winter. Some pretty fancy explaining would have to be done to Mom on that score, too, I realized.

But none of Dad's labor-saving notions would have been so bad, I mean I could have coped with them, at least, if it hadn't been for that darned Comprehensive Schedule he had tacked to the kitchen bulletin board and which I was supposed to follow to the letter.

Talk about Simon Legree with his big whip, that's what the Schedule amounted to. The idea of having a definite day and a definite hour to do each household task may be okay in theory but it is a terrific headache in practice. Every time I was a little late getting home from school, I'd find that my various tasks had sort of telescoped, so that there was an impossible number of them to do in far too little time. Then I'd have a mad hectic scramble to catch up. I even pressed Brose into service after school on Wednesdays, when I was supposed, according to the Schedule, to "defrost refrigerator (4 o'clock), burn trash and contents of waste baskets in rubbish burner (4:15), sweep porches and steps (4:30), start dinner (5:00)."

Brose practically always burned the rubbish and swept the porches for me. He didn't seem to mind. It was the only way we could possibly squeeze in an occasional malted at Joe's. Because every day of the week was just as full of scheduled tasks as Wednesday. Honestly, I don't see how Dad thought them all up. And he took such pride and delight in checking up and finding that I'd done all the jobs he'd figured out for me, that I didn't have the heart to break down and tell him his male ideas about housekeeping were driving me simply nuts.

It wasn't that I wouldn't have got everything done, either, if I'd been left to my own bumbling female system. I'm sure I'd have managed. But I began to look on the Schedule as a hated enemy. And the fact that I couldn't come right out and say so without hurting Dad's feelings sort of gnawed at me inside.

Once Brose asked me, as we were walking home from school, "What's wrong, Tobey? You act as if you're brooding over something."

"I am," I admitted. "That darned Schedule of Dad's is getting me down."

"Getting you down?" Brose asked incredulously. "Why, I think it's terrific."

"You would," I said dully.

"I'll bet you couldn't manage at all without it," Brose argued. "Why, your father was telling me just last night he's figured his methods save you an approximate two hundred and twenty-seven steps a day."

"No!" I exclaimed with pardonable sarcasm. "I thought it was only two hundred and twenty-three!"

Brose gave me a pained look. He said, "I don't think you appreciate all the time and effort your father's put into the Schedule, Tobey."

"I've put time and effort into it, too," I griped.

Brose said reprovingly, "You don't have the proper attitude at all."

I laughed hollowly. "Wait till Mom gets home," I said. "Wait till you see her attitude."

Chapter Fourteen

DAD HANDLES EVERYTHING

JANET's baby was born on the seventeenth of January. It was another boy. Isn't that always the way? Our family runs entirely to girls and apparently Janet's is going to be vice versa. They named him Stephen, which has always been one of my very favorite names. I think names are terribly important. Take poor Brose, who was actually christened Ambrose. A thing like that could simply warp a person's life, if he wasn't a good enough fighter to make the other kids start calling him by some nickname at an early age. For that matter, take me, whose first name is Henrietta, after my father. I mean if I hadn't had a fairly bearable middle name to use instead—well, what would I have done?

Anyway, it was a relief to know the baby had actually arrived. Now surely Mom would be home before long. If I could hold out a few more weeks, she could cope with Dad and his darned old Schedule and I wouldn't have to back down on my word.

But, as it worked out, Fate stepped in to save me even sooner. Only at first, as is so often the way, I didn't recognize it as Fate at all. It just seemed like a bad case of sniffles and sneezes on my part. Then I started feeling hot one minute and cold the next, so Dad got scared and called the doctor. That was on Saturday and Midge had to phone Brose and break my date with him that night, because by then Dr. Merrill had diagnosed my illness as flu and had ordered me to bed. I felt too terrible to argue, although I do vaguely remember babbling something about the Schedule and not knowing who was going to carry it out.

Dad told me not to worry. He said confidently, "I'll take care of everything, baby. It's just lucky I had my

System all worked out before this happened. Now I can take over without any trouble at all. You just concentrate on getting well. That's the important thing."

"But you won't be here," I argued hoarsely. "You'll have to go to work. And Midge—"

"Stop fretting," Dad said firmly. "I'll stay home from work till you're better. Midge and I will get along fine."

All the next week I had to stay in bed and take tons of pills and drink gallons of liquids. At first I felt too utterly miserable to care what was going on in the rest of the house. But as my temperature went down, my curiosity as to how Dad was getting along increased. It seemed to me there were an awful lot of bumps and thumps and loud profane exclamations from downstairs. And once all the lights went off and the electric clocks stopped and it turned out Dad had blown a fuse trying to fix the toaster, which had got knocked off the table when he tripped over the cord. Midge complained to me through a crack in the door, which was how we carried on conversations while I was still germy, that the food was terrible.

"Are you telling me?" I answered. "I eat here, too, you know."

"Yes, but even Dad can't spoil canned soup and fruit and stuff like that," Midge said sorrowfully. "You should taste what he does to meat and veg'tables." She lowered her voice to a discreet whisper. "He's a lots worse cook than you."

"Well, thanks," I said. I asked then, practically whispering, too, "How's everything aside from the cooking?"

Midge heaved a deep sigh. "A mess," she confided. "But don't tell Dad I said so. He doesn't want you worried."

"What kind of a mess?" I probed for more information.

Midge admitted, "Well, the sink's clear full of dirty dishes. And something kind of sticky got spilled on the kitchen floor and we walked in it. But we can't scrub the kitchen till Friday, according to the Schedule, so—"

"The dishes are supposed to be washed every day, though," I objected.

"I know," Midge admitted. "But Dad's got sort of behind with lots of things. It took him a whole afternoon to fix over that shelf-business he keeps the pans on near the stove."

"Why did it have to be fixed?" I asked.

"That day Dad tripped over the toaster cord, he sort of fell into the pans and broke the shelf."

I nodded. That must have been Wednesday. I remembered having heard the crash.

"Where's Dad now?" I asked.

"Down on the couch," Midge informed me, "kind of resting. He says housework's more tiring than he realized." Her voice sank a confidential note lower. "He spent a lot of time last night trying to revise the Schedule."

"You mean," I couldn't suppress a little giggle, "he's willing to admit there are any flaws in it?"

"Not out loud," Midge said, "but he was using some bad words while he was working on it."

We heard Dad's voice then, calling from downstairs, "Midge—Midge, where are you?"

"Up here," Midge called back, "talking to Tobey through the door."

"I want you to go to the store," Dad told her. "There are a couple of little things I forgot when I shopped."

Midge sighed abysmally. "You *always* forget something," she complained, clumping down the stairs.

Now that I was feeling a little better, I began to worry about getting behind with my school work. But Dr. Merrill said I must stay in bed a few more days. So Brose brought some of my books home. He had been wonderfully thoughtful and attentive, calling up every day to find out how I was, even sending me a lovely bouquet that must have set him back practically his whole allowance.

It wasn't too bad having to stay in bed, now that I felt like reading and listening to the radio. I did my nails till they were absolutely perfect and thinned out my eyebrows a teeny bit. I experimented with hairdos and caught up on my homework assignments and exchanged notes with Barbie Walters with Midge acting as messenger. All in all life was quite pleasant and effortless. And the realization that, as long as I kept to my bed, I wouldn't be a slave to Dad's Schedule, made me very content to pamper myself a little, just as the doctor said I should.

Midge kept me posted on poor Dad's progress as a cook and housekeeper, if you could call it progress. The climax came on Saturday, which, I distinctly recalled, involved a notation on the Schedule that read "clean house (9:00 to 11:30)."

Well, Dad was on his way downstairs, bearing the dust mop and vacuum cleaner and his special kit of paraphernalia that I knew so well, when he tripped and fell. The crash brought me out of bed in a leap, although I was definitely unsteady on my feet and my knees felt like limp bath towels in that awful way flu leaves you for a while. I staggered to the head of the stairs and looked down on a writhing heap made up of my father, all the cleaning equipment, the stair window curtain, which he had grabbed at for support in mid-flight and a few other oddments. Dad was holding his ankle and moaning and using strong language in the same breath, so I could see he hadn't been killed. Midge was wringing her hands and crying and asking what she could do.

"Call the doctor," I ordered, sitting down weakly on the top step before my knees gave way entirely.

"You get back to bed," Dad ordered, scowling up at me. "I've just sprained my ankle, or broken it—I'm not quite sure which. But it won't help matters any for you to have a relapse."

Midge ran to call Dr. Merrill. And she must have made it sound urgent, all right, because he was there inside of a few minutes, black bag in hand, puffing, but competent.

"All right, now," he said, brushing aside all the cleaning paraphernalia that was still practically submerging my father. "Let's have a look at you."

100

He caught a glimpse of me then, still huddled at the head of the stairs. "Go back to bed," he told me comfortingly. "Don't you know this old bird's too tough to exterminate?"

Dr. Merrill and my father are good friends and golf partners and they always insult each other that way. I decided he must not consider Dad's injuries too serious, so I wobbled back to bed and pulled the covers up around me. My teeth were chattering with what must have been delayed shock. After a short while I felt better, only anxious to know how badly Dad was hurt.

As it turned out, his ankle was merely sprained, not broken. The doctor took care of it, then helped him to bed. A few days off his feet should fix him up fine, Dr. Merrill said. So he proceeded to get hold of Mrs. Clyde, who does practical nursing and has been a tower of strength to our family in several previous emergencies.

Mrs. Clyde moved in that very afternoon and took things into her plump capable hands in a big way. In less time than it takes to tell it, she had the household running as smoothly as it does when Mom's home, and this in spite of having two invalids to take care of.

After she had Dad and me all comfortable and had given us our lunches, she and Midge ate in the kitchen. I could hear my little sister's voice droning on and on, so I guess she told Mrs. Clyde all about things in general and the Comprehensive Schedule for Efficient Homemaking in particular.

Anyway, a little later, I saw Mrs. Clyde's ample figure move past my bedroom door. She seemed to be on her way to see Dad and she had something that looked like the Schedule in her hand.

"Now what's all this nonsense?" I heard her asking Dad in her rich Scottish brogue. "This list of tasks and duties and whatever? No woman can do her work according to a list of rules and regulations long as my arm. What are ye tryin' to do, make slaves of us then?"

Dad sounded so cowed, I couldn't make out exactly what he answered. But I could tell that he felt he was in no position to take a chance on Mrs. Clyde up and quitting. Or maybe he just wasn't so enthusiastic about the Schedule himself, now that he'd had to jump at its bidding whether he felt like it or not.

I could hear the sharp decisive sound of paper tearing and Mrs. Clyde's firm voice saying, "Good, then. I'll just get rid of this silly thing and forget about it. And another thing I wanted to ask ye. What's that monstrosity settin' by the stove, takin' up good space and making an untidy shambles of Mrs. Heydon's nice neat kitchen?"

Again Dad's reply was a mere mumble. And he didn't argue a speck when Mrs. Clyde went on, "If it's all the same to you, then, it'll make fine kindlin' to start a fire in the fireplace, as I was just thinkin' of doin', it bein' a bit chilly today."

"Tobey," Midge's voice was a whisper outside my door, "you hear that?"

"I certainly did," I whispered back.

Already I was feeling surprisingly better. I only wished I'd thought to ask Dr. Merrill if I couldn't possibly get up the next day.

Chapter Fifteen

BARBIE'S PARTY

BY THE time I had quite recovered and was back in school and we were able to get along without Mrs. Clyde's help, she had managed to efface all evidence of Dad's System from the house and our lives. I was a little afraid he might want me to start in on it again, but he didn't. I guess the week he spent resting his ankle and reading detective stories gave him time to think things over. And he voiced the result of his thoughts to me one night shortly before Mom was expected home.

"I have decided," Dad said, "that housework is woman's natural province and that men, even though they may have ideas that are more basically sound and logical, had just as well keep their noses out of the matter."

"I tried, Dad," I said apologetically. "Honestly, I did. It was just that the Schedule was—well, it was like some sort of Creature breathing down my neck all the time. I couldn't seem to keep ahead of it and it gave me a kind of futility complex or something. But I wouldn't have had the heart to simply toss it aside, the way Mrs. Clyde did."

"I know," Dad nodded. He looked sad for a moment, then he appeared to brighten. "But maybe it's just as well."

"What do you mean?" I asked.

"Your mother," Dad confided. "I'm sure she'd have reacted to the Schedule just as Mrs. Clyde did. Women are so—" he groped for a word, "so tradition-bound."

I didn't think it was quite the right word. I felt "realistic" would have described it better. But there was no use being nasty about it.

"Even you, Tobey," Dad went on in a tone of mellow regret. "Young as you are and open-minded, still I could tell you were just going along with my ideas to humor me."

"I didn't know it showed," I said gently.

Dad chuckled. "Well, anyway, it's all over now. And you've turned out to be quite a good cook and you're taking the housework in stride like a veteran. So I guess no harm's been done."

"None at all," I agreed.

"There's just one thing," Dad said sort of hesitantly. "I've decided there's no point in telling your mother anything about the Schedule when she gets back."

"Oh?" My voice went up a little in surprise.

"After all," Dad went on, "women are sensitive in the strangest ways. She might take it as a reflection on her abilities as a housekeeper for me to have tried to work out an improved system at all. You see what I mean?"

So we passed the word along to Midge and Brose and they agreed not to tell Mom anything about Dad's Comprehensive Schedule. And none of us ever did. Everything was running comparatively smoothly by the time she got home. And, except for my flu and Dad's sprained ankle, Mom never knew we'd had a bit of trouble all the time she'd been away.

She was so full of news about the new baby and little Jimmy, she hardly gave us a chance to talk, anyway. According to Mom, there never were children like them. And she told us all about Janet's and Jim's cute ranch-type home and how happy they were. It seemed as if the visit had helped Mom as much as Janet. I guess grandmothers are like that.

February dragged along, all slush and drizzle as usual. Barbie planned a terrific Valentine party, with each couple told to come dressed as famous lovers in fact or fiction. Brose and I had a hard time making up our minds who we'd be. We discarded all the obvious ones, like Romeo and Juliet, Antony and Cleopatra, and Mickey and Minnie Mouse. For a while we thought we'd go as Adam and Eve, in long underwear and lots of leaves, but Mom thought that was a bit extreme. Secretly, I was just as glad, since I preferred something more glamorous in the way of a costume. Finally I suggested Lillian Russell and Diamond Jim Brady.

At first Brose objected. "I thought they were just good friends. They never got married, did they?"

"No," I admitted, "but they went everywhere together. People always mention them in the same breath. Besides," I hurried on persuasively, "the costumes would be easy to work out. You can always turn up a lot of Gay Nineties stuff in people's attics."

I didn't consider this just the time to add that I knew the very attic. Brose might think I was prejudiced if he learned Midge had already felt out Miss Tess Wentworth for me and had discovered that Miss Tess would be glad to loan me anything I wanted out of the trunks she had stored away.

Brose said, with a little chuckle, "My father's got a

suit of evening clothes that looks like the Gay Nineties."

"There you are," I said, keeping my fingers crossed. "See how easy it would be? I'll bet we could find you a fancy satin vest. And you could buy lots of glass jewelry at the dime store."

Brose shook his head regretfully. "The suit's too big around for me. You know how heavy Dad always has been."

"Use some stuffing," I suggested. "Diamond Jim was a big eater, remember? He was pretty heavy, too."

"Yeah," Brose said and it was plain to see he was warming to the idea, "I suppose I could do that." He asked me then, "But are you sure you could turn up something suitable?"

"Just leave it to me," I said.

Men are so easy to manipulate, if you just go at it in the right way . . .

Miss Tess' attic proved even better than I'd hoped. She wouldn't attempt the narrow third-floor stairs herself, but she sent Midge and me up and told us to help ourselves to whatever we wanted to borrow. It was chill and cheerless up there under the sloping roof, with only the light of a single unshaded bulb overhead. But it seemed as if Miss Tess had never thrown anything away, so our search proved short and fruitful.

Not only did I turn up an emerald velvet dress, with a very low neckline and a perfectly darling little bustle, but a black velvet picture hat as well, with a coquettish ostrich plume. There was a cinnamon moire, too, which was quite fetching, but I thought the velvet looked more Lillian-Russell-ish. Once I had decided on it for sure, Midge and I both turned our attention to augmenting Brose's costume. We found him a brocaded vest in shades to shame the rainbow, and even a high silk hat, one of the collapsible kind that would be sure to tickle him silly.

When we descended the stairs with our loot, Miss Tess invited us to have tea with her. And we did, sitting in her elegant drawing room in front of a smouldering cannel coal fire. She was so cute, telling us all about the ball for which she had bought the emerald velvet dress, and the small sensation she had created, because bustles were very new then.

"And just a little shocking," Miss Tess admitted with a small reminiscent smile. "I remember Papa was rather provoked with me. But the young men liked it. My dance card was quite full."

As her precise voice continued, answering some question of Midge's, I found my thoughts wandering just a little. Why hadn't Miss Tess ever married, I reflected. Judging by the portrait over the tall marble mantel, the one Midge had told me of once, Miss Tess had been quite a beauty in her day. Was there a broken heart, a lover lost in a war, a tragic romantic affair of some sort in her background? It was one of those things I'd never know, still it was sort of thrilling to think about.

When tea was over and it was starting to grow dusky outside, I told Midge I thought we'd better go. So Miss Tess had her housekeeper wrap up the clothes I had chosen and I thanked her for letting me take them.

"It's a pleasure to have them used again, my dear," Miss Tess said warmly. "You'll be very lovely in that gown."

It was the sort of compliment that usually made me feel a little silly and ill at ease. But now I said, without a moment's hesitation, "Thanks, but I won't be half as lovely as you were when you wore it."

And I meant it, too . . .

Still, I must admit that Brose's eyes sort of popped when I came downstairs the night of Barbie's party. Up in my room, putting the final touches on my costume, I had heard Midge and my parents exclaiming over the sight of Brose in all his glory.

"Now that," I had heard my father say, "is what used to be referred to as 'a fine figure of a man.'"

"You're not just kidding, Mr. Heydon," Brose had answered, chuckling. "But I have to admit only about half of it is me. The rest's some old drapes of my mother's

I used for stuffing. But wait till you get a load of this trick hat."

I was all ready by that time, but I waited for their laughter over the collapsible opera hat to subside before I went slowly and langorously down the stairs. It was such a wonderful chance to make an entrance. Who wouldn't take advantage of it?

I had managed to curl my bangs into a reasonable facsimile of a pompadour and had done my back hair high on my neck in a froth of curls. This made my wide plumed hat seem quite at home. The green velvet dress was positively swoony, leaving my throat and shoulders bare and sweeping down around my ankles in rich folds. Mom had said I might use any of the quaint old-fashioned jewelry Grandmother Tobey, for whom I had been named, had left us. So I had chosen a cameo pendant on a thin gold chain and gold eardrops set with tiny pearls.

"G-gosh," was all Brose seemed able to say when he saw me. "Gosh, Tobey—" But the expression on his face was so dazzled, I didn't mind his being at a loss for words.

Even my father was impressed. "Women really knew how to make the most of their charms in those days," he said admiringly. "Wish I'd been around then."

"That'd make you your own grand-paw," Midge chortled.

"You do look nice, dear, only—" Mom frowned slightly. "Did they really wear dresses that low-cut in the nineties?"

"Must have," I told her. "This is an authentic museum piece, remember? Anyway," I added to put her mind at ease, "it's got little concealed stays, so you don't have to worry."

"Well, good," Mom said relievedly.

When we were out in the car, Brose told me, "Gee, Tobey, you're sensational! When I saw you coming downstairs—well, it gave me a queer feeling. I mean, you looked so beautiful, so poised, it was almost as if you were someone I didn't know."

"Why, thank you," I murmured, feeling a little flustered at the compliment. "I'm really just the same little old funny-face you usually pick up at this address."

"Yeah," Brose said. "Yeah! *Now* I remember. Only don't go so gorgeous and remote on me again," he warned, starting the motor. "It scares me."

Barbie's party was sensational. First of all everyone had to guess what pair of lovers each couple represented and there was a prize for the two whose costumes were voted the best. Brose and I won by a very flattering majority. Since it proved to be a pair of tickets to the movies, we had no problem of splitting it up. Next we played all sorts of corny sentimental games, Post Office and A-Tisket A-Tasket and Hearts. After that the party sort of settled down to dancing, as most of our crowd's parties seem to.

It was during this latter portion of the evening that a thing happened which was to have a profound effect on my future, although I had no idea of it at the time.

Partly to fill in a void left by Pete Palmer's having broken his leg ice-skating and so being unable to come, and partly, I suspected, because she had long nourished a secret yen to know him better, Barbie had invited Kim Fairbanks to her party. I knew Kim, of course, although he had never been one of our special crowd. Next to Red Anderson, the captain of the football team, Kim was probably the most outstanding man in the senior class. He was very brilliant, inclined to be moody sometimes, but definitely attractive in a dark, smooth, poised sort of way. He was president of the Drama Club, of which I was only one of the minor members, and had actually got a job doing small parts with a summer theater during vacation. Because of his acting talent Kim always got good parts in the school plays. Lots of girls I knew had crushes on him. And, to be perfectly frank, it did sort of make your heart do a loop when he turned his dark, rather searching eyes in your direction. I wasn't entirely immune myself, although he had never paid enough attention to me to convince me he knew I was around.

But tonight was different.

Kim had come in modern evening clothes and Linda Mason, his date, wore a sophisticated formal and had her hair done in a rather extreme manner. It had been awfully hard to guess who they represented, but it turned out to be Alfred Lunt and Lynn Fontanne. I was pretty sure this had been Kim's idea, as it was far too original to have been thought up by Linda.

Anyway, all evening long I was aware of Kim's stirring dark glance following me about. And the first time we danced together, he told me, "Tobey, that costume simply transforms you. Your whole personality is changed."

"Why, thank you, Kim," I managed. Brose had said much the same thing, but it sounded more exciting on Kim's lips.

He went on in his low, curiously personal voice that made you feel singled out and special, "Tonight you're a woman, a warm, beautiful, desirable woman, with all a woman's wiles and graces, able to lift a man to the heights or drive him to the depths."

Kim could say things like that without sounding corny or affected. It was the way he said them, as though he were speaking lines from a play, making you feel like the heroine, instead of just a girl, dancing at a party. I smiled up at m and felt his arm pull me just a little closer.

I said softly, "It's only the clothes. I'm not any different tonight than any other time."

"Then I've been blind," Kim's breath stirred the hair over my ear. "Tobey," he went on, his voice curiously urgent and intense, "you know our class play this year is laid in the nineties. You'd be absolutely perfect as the heroine, Lady Isobel."

"I—I would?" I repeated, not very intelligently. But I'd never been the leading lady in a play yet. So the idea was a little startling.

"Yes," Kim said firmly, "I'm sure of it. So sure that I wish you'd let me coach you just a little before the try-outs next week. Then you could cinch it, I know."

"But—but wouldn't that be a lot of bother for you?" I asked, hardly believing my own ears. Kim Fairbanks, the

Big Wheel, the aloof and elusive, offering to coach me!

"Bother!" Kim's disturbing glance was deep on mine, his faint smile quizzical. "It will be a pleasure—Lady Isobel..."

Chapter Sixteen

KIM GIVES ME POINTERS

NATURALLY I said nothing to Brose about Kim's offer to coach me. For one thing, Kim might do nothing further about it and then I'd look pretty silly if I'd talked too soon.

But Monday afternoon Kim caught up with me in the school corridor as I was hurrying to Biology and said, "Tobey, if you aren't busy tonight I'd like to drop over and run through that part with you. I've got a couple of ideas about it that I think might help you put it over big in the tryouts Friday."

"That'll be fine," I said, rather breathlessly, and not entirely because I'd been hurrying so fast, either. "Just fine."

So when Brose and I walked home together later, with our usual stopover at Joe's for a hot fudge sundae, I kept my fingers crossed, hoping Brose wouldn't be planning to come over that night. But no such luck, of course. Life always has to be so complicated.

Brose said enthusiastically, "I got a lot of folders and stuff about college, Tobey. How about me bringing them over tonight to show you? Maybe you'll decide to go to Colorado, too."

"I'll be lucky to get to go to Central," I said. "When you have four daughters to put through school, like my parents have, you don't send them so far from home it takes a lot of money for transportation."

"Yeah, but you could look at the stuff about Colorado, anyway," Brose argued. "It's interesting. And don't you want to know what it's like where I'm going?"

"I'd love to," I told him. "But—not tonight."

His glance got a little suspicious. "What's the matter with tonight?"

I had no choice then but to admit, "Well, I'm going to be busy."

"Doing what?" Brose pressed.

So I told him, "Kim Fairbanks is coming over to give me some pointers for the class play tryouts."

"Kim Fairbanks?" Brose repeated incredulously. "That big ham?"

"He is not," I said hotly. "He has more acting talent in his little finger than you have in your whole body!"

"I *know* I'm no actor," Brose said. "And, would you believe it, I don't even care. It's a crummy profession, if you ask me. Nobody but a big sissy—"

"Actors are *not* sissies!" I said scathingly. "You're just saying that because you know you wouldn't have a chance to get a part in the tryouts and Kim will be practically sure to snag the lead." A sudden wonderful thought struck me. If Kim got the leading man's part in the class play and I got to be Lady Isobel, we'd be playing all the romantic scenes opposite each other! And there were a lot of romantic scenes in *Never Tomorrow*.

"He's welcome to it!" Brose snapped. "I think the play committee was nuts to choose a turkey like that, anyway! Why couldn't they decide on a good musical, or at least a comedy, instead of that heavy mid-Victorian dramatic drivel?"

"You simply have no appreciation of serious drama," I informed him. "*Never Tomorrow's* wonderful, practically a classic."

"All the girls can have a good cry over it," Brose snorted callously. "And all the guys'll be bored stiff, except maybe a few high-brows like Kim Fairbanks and his loony crowd."

"You're simply showing your ignorance when you talk that way," I told him cuttingly. "You make it sound as if it's some sort of disgrace to be an intellectual."

"If they're intellectual, I'm glad I'm a moron," Brose said in a Mortimer Snerd-ish sort of tone.

Honestly, he can be so exasperating! We had reached our front walk then, so I said coldly, "Give me my books, please."

And Brose handed them to me with a very mean scowl and said, "Gladly!" He stalked off without even saying good-bye, so I knew he was really burned up. But I didn't care. I was pretty burned up, myself . . .

When Kim came over that night, I wasn't quite ready. I had decided to wear my black velveteen skirt and beige jersey blouse, since the blue jeans and T-shirt I had got into after school hardly seemed appropriate for a potential Lady Isobel. So I was still upstairs when the bell rang and I heard my father go a bit grumblingly along the hall to answer it. I was glad I had mentioned at dinner that Kim was coming. Otherwise, I could just imagine my father saying, "Oh, I thought it was Brose when I heard the doorbell. It usually is."

To my utter horror, I heard my father's surprised voice downstairs saying, "Oh, I supposed it would be Brose. It usually is."

I realized then that he hadn't heard a word I'd said about Kim coming over. Isn't that just like a parent? They don't pay a bit of attention to the important things you tell them, but anything trivial makes a terrific impression.

I heard Mom call from the living room, "Henry, have him come in. Tobey's expecting him. She told us they were going to practice for some play."

At least, I thought with a sigh of relief, Mom could be depended on. I proceeded to brush my hair and put on some lipstick without too much anxiety as to what might be going on downstairs.

When I reached the living room some ten minutes later, I found that I needn't have worried at all. My father and Kim were deep in a discussion of the effect of the discovery of atomic energy on modern youth. My father looked as if he might be a little beyond his depth and poor Mom seemed quite confused, but Kim was perfectly at ease and apparently had a wealth of profound ideas on the subject. He is really *very* brilliant.

He appeared glad to see me, though, and I could tell by his appreciative glance that my change of clothes was making exactly the right impression. I thought my parents seemed a little relieved when I suggested that we could rehearse better in the library.

Kim said, "An excellent idea. I got hold of a copy of the script."

So we went into the library and sat down on the couch and for the first half hour, Kim told me just what his conception of Lady Isobel's character was. It was terribly thrilling to listen. Kim could really make you see things and feel things. A couple of times I actually found myself with tears in my eyes.

Kim noticed and said, "I knew you were sensitive, capable of feeling emotions deeply. I want very much for you to get the part, Tobey. I feel you'd be exactly right in it."

"Do you, Kim, really?" I asked.

He nodded and for a breathless moment he laid his hand over mine. "That's why I'm trying to help you get the feel of the character, to understand what motivates her, what makes her tick. There'll be a mob of girls reading lines at the tryouts, but you can get the part if you really try. Miss Jefferson will have the final say, of course, as head of the English department. But the play committee's opinion will carry quite a bit of weight with her and I think I can get them pulling for you."

"I don't see why you're going to all this trouble for me," I told him, my heart beating fast.

He released my hand with a little, knowing smile. "Don't you? Maybe it's just that I like to discover new talent," he said. "Or it could be because you looked the part so perfectly in that costume you wore at the party."

"But maybe I'm not a good enough actress." My voice quavered just a little.

"You are," Kim said firmly. "Never doubt yourself. Shall we run through some of the lines now?"

"Oh, yes," I breathed.

Kim asked then, glancing around the room, "Is that a record player over there?" At my mystified nod, he continued, "Could we put on a few records? Something like—oh, 'Clair de Lune,' some others of that kind. There's nothing like a faint undercurrent of music to induce the proper mood."

So with a softly, gently sad musical background, we proceeded to run through Lady Isobel's lines. They were wonderful, so dramatic and moving. Kim coached me carefully as to just how they should be read. He played the part of Jonathan, giving me my cues. He sounded absolutely professional.

"Do you think you'll get the Jonathan part?" I asked.

Kim quirked an eyebrow, exactly the way I've seen it done in the movies. "Know anybody who's likely to take it away from me in the tryouts?" he asked quizzically.

It would have sounded like bragging from anyone else, but the way Kim said it, as if he were sort of poking fun at himself, took away the sting.

"No, I can't," I admitted.

We worked hard all that evening. But it was the most stimulating sort of work I had ever done.

Brose was simply furious when he heard that Kim was coming over the next night to coach me, too. We argued all the way home from school, not even taking time to stop at Joe's. Finally, when we reached our front walk, I demanded, "What right have you to get so mad? We didn't have a date till Wednesday. And I'm not breaking that."

"That's white of you," Brose gritted. "Mighty white!"

"Unless you'd prefer to break it," I said coldly.

Brose shook his head. "I wouldn't." He added so plaintively that I found myself feeling sorry for him, "But what about my French?"

After all, I couldn't let him flunk, even if practically all I could think of was the play tryouts and whether I'd really be able to land the leading feminine part.

"Okay," I conceded, smiling up at him. "Come in right

114

now and I'll help you with your assignment for tomorrow."

"Gee, will you, Tobey?" Brose said gratefully, his earlier rage apparently under control.

But when we got inside the front door, Mom called from the kitchen, not realizing I wasn't alone, "Tobey, Kim dropped off some books about the theater for you. He thought maybe you'd have a chance to skim through them before tonight."

"Thanks," I called back, "I'll look at them later."

When I glanced up at Brose he was scowling. "What's that would-be Hamlet trying to do?" he demanded belligerently.

"He's simply helping me learn a few pointers about acting," I said soothingly. "He wants me to get the leading woman's part in the play."

"Why?" Brose asked nastily.

"Because he feels I have talent," I said, lifting my chin. "He says when he saw me in that costume at Barbie's it was as if Lady Isobel had come to life before his eyes."

"Oh, he did, did he," Brose growled. "Sounds to me as if he's trying to muscle in on my girl. And I don't like it!"

"Oh, Brose," I said, feeling my heart beat a little faster at the thought, "he hasn't any interest in me personally. It's just my acting."

"I'll bet," Brose said. "That wolf!"

We went into the library and I proceeded to help him with his French. "I really think you could do this yourself," I told him. "You've got a complex about it now—or else it's just that I've helped you so much you've come to depend on me."

"Maybe you'd like to stop," Brose said, "so you could devote all your time to the theatah?"

"Very funny!" I said.

"Maybe you could understudy Tallulah Bankhead after Kim gets through giving you some more priceless advice."

"All right," I snapped, "be a blight! It seems to come naturally for you."

"Aw, gee, Tobey," Brose caught my hand but I pulled

115

free. "Can't you see through that phony? He only thinks he's a great actor."

"That," I said coldly, "is your opinion."

"It sure is," Brose agreed, but he evidently realized he had pushed me as far as he'd better.

Because he dropped the subject of Kim Fairbanks as of that moment and didn't bring it up again. He even said a very sweet thing just as he was ready to leave.

He told me, "If you really want to snag that part in the play, I hope you make it, Tobey."

"Why, thanks, Brose," I said.

"And you don't need any coaching, either," he added. " 'Bye, now. See you tomorrow."

He can really be very nice when he wants to. The only trouble is, he so often doesn't want to.

Chapter Seventeen

MAN TROUBLE

MY FATHER inquired plaintively at breakfast, "Is this new fellow going to be around all the time now? Two nights in a row you've had a date with him. Isn't that rushing things a little?"

Honestly, parents can be so dense sometimes. I opened my mouth to explain that Kim and I hadn't had a single date, that his coming over had been in a purely professional capacity.

But before I could get the words out, Midge said through a mouthful of toast, in her revolting way, "Brose doesn't like it, either. He argued with Tobey something awful yesterday while she was doing his French."

"Eavesdropper!" I hissed at her.

"I am not!" Midge denied indignantly. "Me and Judy could hear you plain out on the stairs where we were playing horses. Brose said—"

"It's none of your business anyway," I informed her.

Then, to my father who had started all this, I explained the true purpose of Kim's visits.

"How nice of him," Mom said when I had finished. She poured some more coffee for my father. "Do you think you'll get the part, dear?"

"The tryouts are Friday. I won't know till next week." My father sighed.

"Just what does that mean?" I inquired.

"Nothing," Dad said, "only—well, Brose is so much easier to talk to. With him I can relax while we discuss sports and kindred low-brow subjects. Kim gets me involved in atomic energy and foreign policy and the comparative abilities of Ibsen and Shaw. He's considerably more wearing on the brain."

"Kim is very smart," I informed my father. "He's a wonderful actor, too. You should appreciate all the time and effort he's spending on me."

"Oh, I do," my father said, too gravely.

"Now, Henry, don't tease," Mom admonished. "Naturally Tobey would like to be the leading lady in the class play. And if Kim can help her, the least we can do is co-operate."

"I suppose so," Dad said. "But Brose is definitely the lesser of two evils . . ."

I didn't see how I could possibly live through the play tryouts, with Miss Jefferson, all busty and bustling, in charge and the three members of the play committee sitting in. The big auditorium stage was stark and cheerless in the feeble late afternoon sunshine. Certainly all illusion of a theater was missing. I could feel my knees bumping together as I began reading the Lady Isobel part. Could I remember all the tips Kim had given me, the little nuances of voice and inflection he had said were so vital? Now there was no faint background music to help create a mood, I had to do it all alone. And although I relaxed a little as I got into the feeling of the lines, I didn't think I'd done a good job at all until I happened to catch Kim's eye just as I finished. He smiled at me, his wonderful warm smile, and made a tiny unobtrusive circle with his thumb and forefinger. My heart lifted. Maybe I hadn't been too terrible after all.

Several other girls tried out for the same part, including Mary Andrews. I felt a mean hope that if I didn't get it, she wouldn't, either. I don't know what it is about Mary that rubs me the wrong way. Maybe the fact that she always seems to be just waiting around to grab Brose in case we quarrel has something to do with it. Anyway, I felt she overacted dreadfully.

Kim was simply wonderful as Jonathan. There was no reasonable doubt of his getting the part, none of the other aspirants compared with him. Afterwards, as he walked me home, I told him as much.

"Thanks, Tobey." He gave my hand a little squeeze. "You were pretty wonderful yourself. If you don't play Lady Isobel, I'll eat the script."

I sighed, hoping he was right. If only Miss Jefferson and the play committee shared his opinion!

"How about me dropping over a while tonight?" Kim asked. "I'll bring along some books of poetry. There's nothing like reading poetry aloud," he added, "to improve your diction."

I hesitated. The idea of reading poetry aloud with Kim was so utterly entrancing. Still this was Friday and on Friday nights Brose and I always did something—or *almost* always, some demon of perversity in me corrected. Once in a while something had come up to interfere with our Friday dates, they weren't quite so ironclad as our Saturday ones. And Brose hadn't said anything specific about seeing me tonight. He just *might* not be figuring on it, he'd been so annoyed lately over Kim.

There must be some truth in the old adage that, "He who hesitates is lost," for I found myself murmuring, "Well, yes. I—guess it would be all right, Kim."

This would make four times this week. I wondered what Dad would have to say?

When I got inside the house Mom called questioningly, "Tobey?"

"Yes."

118

"Are you alone?" Mom asked, coming out of the library

"Yes," I said. "Why?"

Mom chuckled. "I just didn't want to get you into another jam, in case Brose was with you." Her tone dipped conspiratorially, even though there wasn't anyone else around. "Dick Allen phoned a little while ago. He's home for the week-end."

"Oh, no!" I moaned.

Mom looked at me in astonishment. "That isn't quite the reaction I expected. I thought you liked Dick."

"I do," I said hollowly, "but why does he have to choose this week-end? It's mixed up enough already!"

I went on to explain and when I had finished Mom said philosophically, "Well, you'll just have to work it out for yourself, dear. But I'm afraid Dick's going to be disappointed if he can't take you out either tonight or tomorrow." She asked then, frowning, "Do you have a definite date with Brose?"

"Well, no," I admitted. "But when you're wearing a boy's class ring, Mom, he naturally expects you to save your Wednesday and Friday and Saturday nights for him."

Mom looked confused. "But you said you were going out with Kim tonight."

"Not going out," I corrected. "We're going to read poetry out loud to each other. It's wonderful for your diction," I explained in response to Mom's increasingly blank look. "So I thought maybe Brose wouldn't be too mad, so long as I wasn't exactly having a date with Kim. But he'd have a fit if I went out with Dick tomorrow night."

After a moment's silence, Mom said quietly, "That class ring seems to be complicating your life quite a bit, doesn't it, Tobey?"

Under the circumstances, how could I deny it?

The week-end was something of a mess. Friday evening was okay, reading poetry with Kim before the blazing log fire. At first the memory of the heated argument

I'd had with Brose on the phone just before dinner bothered me a little. But Kim's moving flexible voice, reading the lovely poems of Robert Frost and William Rose Benét, put all thought of Brose out of my mind. I couldn't read nearly so well, but Kim said I was showing great improvement. The compliment made me practically purr.

Brose was still pretty huffy when we went to the movies Saturday night. He griped so much over Kim that I finally burst out, "Oh, for creep's sake, Brose! If I'd known you were going to be like this, I'd have gone out with Dick instead of wasting my whole evening trying to placate you!"

We were walking home after a hot fudge sundae at Joe's when I said it. Brose stopped dead still to scowl down at me. "Dick!" he exclaimed unbelievingly. "You mean he's around again?"

"Only for the week-end," I told him. "But he asked me to go out. I said no, though, because I had a date with you."

I started walking on and Brose came, too, his feet sloshing angrily through the wet snow. "Fine thing!" he exploded. "I suppose you're going out with him tomorrow instead!"

I said coldly, because I hated being put in a position of having to explain and justify my conduct, "After all, I had to turn him down last night, too."

"That puts him and me in the same boat," Brose growled.

I ignored this. "All I'm going to do is have dinner with him tomorrow. He's leaving at four o'clock."

"Have you two been writing each other?" Brose demanded.

It really wasn't any of his business, but I told him anyway. "No, neither of us is much on writing letters."

"I suppose I have that to be thankful for," Brose said in a very sarcastic tone. "At least, I needn't picture you mooning over a bunch of his letters, tied with a pink ribbon."

"Oh, Brose, you make me so mad!" I snapped.

"Don't you think I get mad?" Brose demanded. "After all, you're supposed to be my girl. And last night you had that drip Fairbanks hanging around. And tomorrow it'll be Allen!"

"Brose, be reasonable," I said. "Dick hasn't been around for months. And Kim—" the mere thought of Kim made me feel a little breathless with excitement, "well, Kim and I have just happened to discover lately that we have a lot of interests in common. The stage," I elaborated, "and—and poetry—"

"Poetry!" Brose snorted. "Holy Sox!"

Because of practically superhuman forbearance and tact on my part, we managed to get through the evening without having a real fight. But it wasn't easy.

By Sunday I was feeling a little limp. Dick drove me away out into the country for early dinner. We went to a rustic inn quite famous around Edgewood for its food and atmosphere. It was very old-English, with thick darkened ceiling beams and tiny-paned windows, a log fire in a great fieldstone fireplace.

Dick didn't say a single word of reproach because I hadn't been able to give him more time. He was really wonderful. He wanted to know all about the class play when I mentioned it. So I told him how Kim had been helping me. "He's only interested in me as an actress," I explained. The thought made me feel sad.

Dick gave me an odd look. "Don't kid yourself. If he wasn't interested in you personally, why would he give a darn whether you got the part or not?"

It was one of those simple truths that are so obvious you can't grasp them just at first. I sat staring at Dick blankly. With his words still echoing in my ears, I realized that Kim must like me. He must like me quite a lot. The thought brought a warm, singing elation in its wake. Because I liked him a lot, too. My heart beat faster and my throat felt all chokey with the thrilling knowledge.

"Do you have to look quite so happy about it?" Dick's wry voice brought me abruptly back to the moment.

"Aren't you satisfied with Brose and me? What's this bird got that we haven't?"

It was sort of funny, hearing him lump himself with Brose, as if they were on one side, as opposed to Kim on the other. And no longer ago than Christmas vacation, Dick and Brose had acted as though they were deadly enemies.

"I haven't got you," I said. "What about all those gorgeous women up at Central?"

"I could forget them if you worked on me a little," Dick said, leaning his elbows on the table.

Even if it was just a line, I enjoyed listening to it. Why did there have to be so many attractive men in the world?

Chapter Eighteen

BREAK-UP

MOMENTOUS happenings occurred during the next few weeks. As I'd hoped, but been afraid to count on, I got the part of Lady Isobel. As everyone had expected, Kim would play Jonathan.

Miss Jefferson called the chosen cast together in the English room after school. "This will mean a great deal of hard work for all of you," she told us in her gushing, high-pitched voice. "But I feel the committee and I have made a good choice. We want this to be the most professional, the most polished play that's ever been produced at Edgewood High."

"We'll certainly do our best," Kim said and the rest of us murmured enthusiastic agreement.

Miss Jefferson nodded, making both her chins quiver, and went on with her pep-talk. "No skimping rehearsals, no slipshod performances. Perfection right down the line to the smallest walk-on. Work, work and more work."

Kim whispered in my ear, "It's going to be the kind of work I enjoy, playing I'm madly in love with you."

I smiled up at him, not daring to risk an answer since Miss Jefferson was frowning warningly in our direction. It was going to be the kind of work I'd enjoy, too, every last entrancing minute of it . . .

Brose was proud and apprehensive at the same time when he heard the news. He said, "I'm glad you got the part, Tobey. I know how much you wanted it—but—well, I wouldn't be telling the truth if I didn't say I'll hate your having so much to do with Fairbanks. I don't trust the guy!"

"That's silly," I said. "Kim's a wonderful person when you get to know him. You just resent him because he's different from you, his interests are all artistic, drama, poetry, things like that. He has a simply terrific mind. Just ask Dad if you don't believe me. And you certainly can't deny he's attractive. And his manners are wonderful, Mom says so, too. He makes a girl feel all—cherished and sort of as if she's on a pedestal. And he says the most flattering things in such a wonderful, serious sort of way—" I broke off at the look on Brose's face, which seemed to be a combination of rage and hurt. "Anyway," I added hastily, "we're just going to be in a play together. That's all."

"You don't sound as if that's all," Brose gulped in a gruff, strangled tone. "You sound like you're falling for the guy. You—you aren't, are you?"

"Of course not," I said positively. But I could feel hot color spreading across my face in a way I hated and had hoped I'd outgrown. My heart was beating so fast I was afraid Brose would notice it under my sweater.

"What you blushing for then?" he demanded.

"Because you're talking such nonsense! It's embarrassing!"

I must have sounded convincing. At least, Brose drew a very deep breath, as though he were relieved. "Well, gee," he said apologetically, "what do you expect me to think? Raving about the big ham that way!"

"Will you stop calling him names?"

Brose frowned. "I might," he said, "if you'd stop talking as though he's something to swoon over."

I sighed. "Let's just drop the subject, shall we?"

"Okay," Brose agreed. "But I'd like it better if we could just drop Kim, preferably on his head . . ."

As days passed and Brose realized how much of my time was going to be taken up with rehearsals, he really hit the ceiling. I pointed out that I couldn't help it, that it was Miss Jefferson's idea and not simply a plot on my part and that of Kim Fairbanks to spend a lot of time together, but it didn't help much.

"I could put up with rehearsals," he grumbled, "even though I hardly ever get to walk you home from school. But when you have to stay in nights, learning your lines and practicing fancy gestures under Fairbanks' expert supervision—well, it's too much!"

"But it's only temporary," I pointed out as patiently as I could. "Once we give the play, things will get back to normal. You'll see."

"I hope I hold out," Brose said morosely.

Only to Barbie Walters, who has been my closest friend since our problems were concerned with hopscotch and skinned knees rather than men, could I confide the whole truth.

"I don't *think* I'm really falling for Kim," I told her one Saturday morning when we were alone in my room setting each other's pin-curls. "But sometimes I'm not—not sure."

Barbie said, "Ouch!" but that was merely because I'd jabbed her with a bobby pin accidentally. Then she said, sighing, "If Kim Fairbanks looked at me the soulful sort of way he does you, I'd fall for him. That dark, dangerous, romantic type really sends me." She shrugged. "So I get Sox, who's tall and blond."

"But how could I fall for Kim," I went on, "when I'm so fond of Brose?"

Barbie's eyes met mine in the dressing-table mirror. "Maybe you aren't really as fond of Brose as you imagine. Maybe he's just got to be a sort of habit with you."

"Oh, no," I shook my head. "I don't like him a bit less than I always did—but—well, Kim makes me feel all—all soft inside and kind of keyed up and excited."

Barbie nodded. "Know what you mean exactly. But," she went on practically, "do you make him feel that way?"

I thought about it for a minute. "He acts as if I do. The way he talks sometimes—" I shut my eyes tight, remembering, "well, it's just like the man in a movie talks to the girl."

"Jeepers," Barbie sighed so deeply that she slumped all over. "The most momentous things happen to you. What are you waiting for?"

"Waiting for?" I repeated, opening my eyes.

"Sure," Barbie said. "If I was wearing Brose's class ring and Kim Fairbanks got interested in me, I'd give it back and say good-bye to Brose so fast it would make his head spin."

Barbie meant well, I knew. But I still wasn't sure what I wanted to do . . .

Never Tomorrow was to be given the second week in April. There would be two performances, Friday and Saturday nights. For weeks ahead we seniors were so busy we were practically running around in circles. Not only the cast, which was rehearsing like crazy. But there were all the committees working on properties and costumes and stage settings and lighting and programs and tickets.

Brose stayed as stubbornly aloof as possible from the whole business, pleading pressure of school work. We had several small scraps over Kim Fairbanks. Somehow my arguments that our interest in each other was purely professional got less and less convincing.

My family wasn't very understanding about the situation, either. Midge called Kim "Glamor-boy" when he wasn't around and I suspected her of spying on us through a crack in the library door when we were rehearsing. My father took to doing urgent little jobs in the basement or upstairs somewhere when Kim came over. And he thought it hilariously funny the day he caught me practicing walking with a big book on my head to improve my posture. Mom was a little better, but even she inquired several times whether I wasn't taking the play too seriously.

When I told Kim of the trouble I was having at home, he was very mature and understanding. He said, "Families can be rough on you, I know. I had a bad time with mine till I made it quite clear that I intended to be an actor and that nothing they could say or do would make any difference. Then they began to take me seriously." He went on to tell me how a lot of famous actors had difficulties convincing their families that the stage was an honorable profession. "Unless you're lucky enough to be born into a family where acting is a tradition, like the Barrymores for instance, it isn't easy to make the stage your career."

I nodded. I hadn't had quite the courage yet to tell Mom and Dad that I meant to be a professional actress. I hadn't known it myself until I got involved in the senior play and found out how utterly fascinating acting was. Kim's concentration and enthusiasm had had a lot to do with it, too, I realized. Why, I found myself thinking, who could tell? Maybe someday Kim and I might be as famous as Sothern and Marlowe, Lunt and Fontanne. As the names of great stage couples drifted through my mind, I realized that most of them were married. I got lost in a heavenly daydream, so that I didn't even hear what Kim was saying. It wasn't until he repeated, "Will you, Tobey?" that I realized he had spoken at all.

"Will I what, Kim?" I asked apologetically. "I'm afraid I was sort of dreaming."

"About me?" Kim asked, his voice so low and thrilling it was like a caress. "If so, I'll forgive you." He went on, "I was saying the Laurence Olivier version of *Hamlet* is showing Saturday over in Hilltown. How about us driving over to see it?"

Saturday, I thought. Would Brose put up with my going out with Kim on Saturday night? But the thought of the twenty-mile drive to Hilltown, of sitting beside Kim through that thrilling performance of Shakespeare, was too entrancing to resist. I would simply have to make Brose understand that this was an opportunity that no one seriously interested in acting could afford to miss.

My voice was a little husky as I threw caution to the winds. "Oh, Kim, I'd love to . . ."

I broke the news to Brose as we lingered in the early spring sunshine outside our house after school the next day. Having it hanging over me any longer was more than I could bear.

I said, "Kim asked me to go see *Hamlet* with him Saturday night. And I said I would. It'll be such a wonderful opportunity to study Laurence Olivier's technique."

Brose didn't say a word for a minute. I looked up to see why and his expression was so furious it jolted me. I'd seen him mad before, but never this mad.

He said, his voice low and sort of deadly, "So now you've begun dating him on Saturdays. May I ask just where that leaves me?"

"Oh, Brose, you don't understand," I began.

But he didn't let me finish. "I understand all right," he said, sticking his jaw out. "It took me longer than it should have, I guess, but I get it now."

I felt sort of gulpy. I'd never seen Brose look like this before, nor heard him sound this way, either. I opened my mouth but no words came out. If they had, they'd only have been drowned out in his angry roar.

"You've fallen for that big phony, hook, line and sinker!" he accused me. "It sticks out all over you. And I thought you had good sense!"

"Brose Gilman, don't you talk to me like that!" I felt my own anger rise to meet his.

"You can't deny you're nuts about him, can you?"

I could have, but would I be telling the truth? Honestly, I wasn't sure myself whether I'd fallen for Kim. I'd only got really acquainted with him such a short time ago and our contacts so far had all been mixed up with the play, with Lady Isobel's undying love for Jonathan. I knew

127

that Kim kept me all stirred up and excited. But I used to get pretty excited over Brose, too, before I knew him so well and got so accustomed to him.

I only wished I could be sure, one way or the other.

Brose taunted, in that sarcastic way that makes me simply boil, "Not saying anything is as good as admitting it!"

"It is not!" I glared at him. "Anyway, you needn't act as if you own me! I've told you all along we aren't really going steady. If I want to have dates with another man, I can!"

"Not," Brose gritted between clenched teeth, "while you're wearing my class ring! You've made a fool out of me long enough!"

"Oh!" I gasped. "Oh!" I was so mad I couldn't think of anything mean and biting enough to say.

Furiously I tugged at his ring. It would choose this time to be hard to get off! Of course, I knew I'd just put too much tape on it, so that it was a little tight. But it almost seemed as if Fate had a hand in it, as if a voice inside me warned, "Take time to think, Tobey. Don't do something you may regret."

I ignored the warning and managed to jerk the hateful ring from my finger. "There it is! I'm sorry I wore it this long!" I flung the ring into his hand.

"Thanks!" Brose said bitterly. His face looked pale and strained and his eyes glittered coldly. "I haven't got yours with me, but you'll have it back just as soon as I can get it to you! It's a shame we wasted so much time on each other!"

He turned and walked down the street with great big steps. I was glad to see him go. And if he never came back, it would be too soon! Now I could date Kim, wonderful, understanding Kim, whenever I wanted to, without feeling guilty over being unfair to Brose. Now I was free. It was a perfectly wonderful sensation.

The tears I could feel welling up into my eyes were due to rage and excitement, nothing more. Nothing whatever more, I told myself as I ran blindly into the house . . .

Chapter Nineteen

SENIOR PLAY

ONCE the first shock was over, I seemed to move through the days that followed my break-up with Brose in a sort of enchanted fog. I was so thrilled with Kim's attentions I had little time for regrets. I couldn't deny I missed Brose. We'd been friends for such a long time and I'd worn his ring for over six months. You can't simply shrug off a relationship like that without some reaction. There were times when I'd be actually lonely for him. Then, when Kim was around, I wouldn't have a thought left over for Brose. It was confusing, trying to unscramble my own emotions. But I didn't have time to worry about it.

For one thing, I was terribly busy with the play. And for another, senior year was no cinch. I really had to spend a lot of time on my studies. How was Brose getting along with his French, I wondered? And then one day after school I saw him and Mary Andrews walking along together conjugating French verbs out loud, so I didn't worry about him any more. Honestly, the way she was mooning up at him was enough to turn your stomach. But Brose didn't seem to mind. Neither of them saw me.

At first, Brose and I were so mad at each other we wouldn't even speak. But that seemed sort of silly as time went on. One day in Math I forgot and asked him something about an assignment and that broke the ice. After that, we were like any other casual acquaintances, say "Hi" when we happened to meet. It was less awkward all around.

Kim didn't walk home from school with me eve the way Brose used to. We agreed such things wer juvenile. But we managed to spend a lot of time The night we went to see *Hamlet* was the first kissed me. It made little pinwheels and skyroc in my veins. I ignored the inner voice that reminded me, "You felt the same way when Brose first kissed you—remember?" But I didn't want to remember. I wanted to concentrate on Kim and how absolutely wonderful he was.

Mom got a little annoyed with me, the way I took to lying on my stomach in front of the record player, listening to "Clair de Lune" over and over.

She said, "Honestly, Tobey, since you broke up with Brose, I don't know what's got into you. You aren't a bit like yourself."

"She's in love," Midge said and made one of her more sickening noises. "She's cuh-razy about Glamor-boy."

"Midge Heydon, don't you dare talk that way!" I sat up, scowling at her.

Dad said in a pained sort of tone, "You're not getting serious over that junior grade Barrymore?"

"I don't see why you all have to be so perfectly mean about Kim!" I glared at everyone indiscriminately. "You didn't want me going steady with Brose and now that I've given him back his ring, you've started picking on Kim. I think you've got some sort of complex!"

"We're not picking on anyone, dear," Mom soothed. "Don't get so worked up."

"She plays that record all the time," Midge put in, "because it's *their* song. I heard them talking about it yesterday."

"Mother," I said, getting to my feet with dignity, "if she doesn't stop listening to my personal private conversations, I—I'll leave home, that's what I'll do!"

I swept upstairs and slammed my bedroom door behind

It was unfortunate that Brose should have picked the next day to try to reason with me. To my surprise to step beside me as I was hurrying home from

your mad rush?" he asked mildly.

've got loads of homework. And there's a rehearsal tonight, so I'll have to get it all done before dinner."

His tone was sort of hesitant, "It wouldn't take too much of your valuable time if I just walked to your corner with you, would it?"

"Not if Mary can spare you," I couldn't resist saying.

Brose scowled. Then he said, "Snooty as you've got lately, I still feel I oughta tell you something I suspect."

"You needn't put yourself out," I assured him. "After all, you don't have to worry about me any more."

"Oh, I don't," Brose said. "But I've known you a long time. We're what you might call old friends. And I'd hate to see Barbie or any other old friend making a dope of herself the way you're doing."

"How kind!" I said scathingly.

Brose said, "Tobey, you've got to listen. That guy's just being sweet to you so you'll get a crush on him and be real good opposite him in the play. It won't be the first time he's pulled a low-down trick like that, either."

"Who says?" My voice shook a little, I was so mad.

"Well—Mary for one," Brose admitted uncomfortably.

"Oh, she does, does she?" I glared at him. "And I suppose you're too blindly infatuated with her to realize she's jealous! I'll bet she's crazy about Kim herself. She tried her darnedest to get the Lady Isobel part and failed. And Kim likes me the best. So she has to make up absolutely fantastic stories—" I broke off, struck by a sudden unbearable thought. "And another thing, Brose Gilman," I snapped, "don't you dare discuss me and my affairs with her again! I won't have it, do you hear?"

"Okay!" Brose glared right back at me. "Okay! Forget I tried to warn you. I should have had more sense than to think you'd listen, the way you're soft in the head over that guy!"

If he hadn't strode on out of my reach just then think I'd have hit him!

The night of the dress rehearsal for *Never Tomor* Kim told me, "Just forget it's a play when I kiss y the end of the second act. It'll be me, Kim, kissin

Tobey. Forget Lady Isobel and Jonathan. Then you won't feel self-conscious about the audience or anything. It'll seem completely real and that will put the scene over."

The rehearsal was a mess, as dress rehearsals always are. But even Miss Jefferson remarked about the realism of that love scene that climaxed the second act. She told Kim and me afterward, "You projected the emotional impact perfectly. I do hope you can do as well when we have an audience."

"We will, won't we, Tobey?" Kim's glance met mine.

And I said, still a little dizzy with the emotional impact of that kiss he had given me, "Oh, yes, Miss Jefferson."

Never Tomorrow proved to be the most sensational senior play that had ever been put on at Edgewood High. Simply everyone said so. The auditorium was packed both nights and the applause practically deafening. We had to take so many final curtain calls I lost count. But Kim didn't. Afterwards he said there had been five curtain calls Friday night and seven on Saturday.

It was quite deflating to learn that Kim was awfully provoked because on Saturday night I got a little mixed up and skipped several lines of dialogue in the third act. He took me to task about it severely at a sort of farewell party the entire cast had at Joe's that night after the play.

"But nobody noticed, Kim," I told him. "I'm sorry, of course, but it really didn't make any difference."

"It could have," Kim said, frowning. "The way you muffed that cue of mine would have thrown anyone else off entirely."

I felt myself coloring. The others were staring at us in surprise. It wasn't very considerate of Kim to make such an issue of my slight mistake. And just when I was feeling like a combination of Helen Hayes and Katherine Cornell, too.

Sox Trevor, who had played the butler, said in an obvious effort to change the subject, "Boy, am I glad it's over. I was scared silly I'd trip myself up in my English bit."

Someone else said, "Miss Jefferson really got into a

132

tizzy, didn't she? All the compliments she was getting went to her head like champagne. I'll bet the poor soul's home in bed with a hang-over already."

The laughter that followed made everybody feel more comfortable. But all the while we were eating our hamburgers and drinking our malteds, I sensed that Kim was still annoyed with me. Honestly, I never knew anyone to make such a mountain out of a molehill!

I told him as much as we lingered on the doorstep after he had taken me home. I said, "I think it's mean of you to act as if I skipped those lines deliberately. No one else thought a thing of it. Even Miss Jefferson said I gave a fine performance."

"Miss Jefferson!" Kim's tone dripped contempt. "What does she know about it? A high school English teacher. If it hadn't been for my suggestions, she'd have bungled the direction badly. You saw how bogged down she got on the last act till I told her—" His voice droned on and on. There was some truth in what he said, of course. He did have a good working knowledge of dramatics. But Miss Jefferson wasn't nearly such a bubble-head as he was making her sound.

I said a trifle coldly, "I don't see why you have to be so critical. The play was a big success."

"It could have been better," Kim insisted. "Now take the way you picked up that letter from the floor in the first act. If you had stooped more gracefully—"

"Oh, for creep's sake!" I exploded. "Didn't I do anything right? Not one teeny little thing?"

"Of course," Kim said. "Your performance seemed all right to an undemanding audience such as we had, made up of doting parents and classmates and teachers. But thought you were serious enough about acting to w the truth."

"Well, I am," I said, "but—"

"If we of the stage don't see our own weaknes mistakes and profit by them," Kim went on, "we reach the top. Acting is a very demanding p there's no room in it for second-raters. It's realize that—" he broke off as I tried to swallow a yawn. "Am I boring you?"

"No, of course not," I told him. "It's just that I'm a little tired. I mean tonight's been so exciting and all."

"In that case," Kim said stiffly, "I won't keep you up any later. Good-night, Tobey."

As he stalked off into the darkness without another word, all the magic went out of the night. I turned and let myself into the house dully ...

With the play off my mind, I settled down to some serious study. I wanted to get my grades high enough so that I could sort of coast through the last weeks of school. There would be so much going on just before graduation, I didn't want to be all tied down with homework. Barbie had the same idea, so we did quite a lot of our studying together, which made it a little less painful.

"What's happened with you and Kim?" Barbie asked bluntly one night when we were relaxing after a particularly tough Math session in her bedroom.

"Well, we're both pretty busy right now." I tried to sound casual. "I haven't been seeing quite so much of him."

"Who," Barbie inquired with her customary brutal but refreshing candor, "are you kidding?"

We sat there, staring at each other. I knew and Barbie, apparently, suspected, that Kim Fairbanks had given me a very fast and humiliating brush-off once the senior play was a thing of the past. He hadn't taken me out a single time. In a way, I was glad Barbie had pinned me down to admitting it, instead of going on trying to put up a good front.

"The stinker!" she exclaimed, when I had confided the whole embarrassing situation. "The unmitigated louse! To think I advised you to give a good Joe like Brose the air for him."

"That wasn't why I did it," I assured her.

Barbie wasn't to blame. Neither was Dick, although he had implanted the idea in my mind that Kim was really interested in me. But a person has to figure things out for herself, whatever others say. And I'd figured wrong. The funny part was, it was mainly my pride that had suffered. My feeling for Kim must have been sheer infatuation. It had collapsed like the angel-food cake I'd tried to bake while Mom was in California. Nor had my burning ambition to go on the stage survived any longer.

I hastened to inform Barbie, "I'm not saying I want Brose back, though. Why, if we made up, I'd have to admit he was right about Kim all along. And I wouldn't humble myself like that."

"I should say not," Barbie agreed staunchly. After a thoughtful moment, she added, "But it's a ghastly time to be caught without a man. There's the Prom coming up and all."

"Yes," I said dully, "I know."

"Brose hasn't given anybody else his class ring," Barbie offered. "I noticed him with it on only yesterday."

"Who cares?" I asked, with a reasonable facsimile of a casual little shrug . . .

Later that night, when I was getting ready for bed, Mom came into my room. She sat on the foot of the bed while I brushed my hair and gave my face a good creaming. Finally she spoke. "Tobey," she asked, her tone troubled, "you wouldn't call me a prying sort of mother, would you?"

"Of course not." I had a good hunch what was coming.

Mom went on, "It seems to both Dad and me lately that you aren't very happy. Is there any way we can help?"

"I'm okay." I managed a little smile. "Thanks, anyway."

Mom asked anxiously, "It wasn't because of anything we said or did that Kim Fairbanks hasn't been around?"

I shook my head.

Mom said, "We've never tried to dictate to our children. We've always felt you should learn to decide things for yourself. That's why we didn't say you couldn't wear Brose's class ring. But we were a little relieved when y gave it back. Not that we don't like Brose," Mom added quickly. "We like him very much, but—"

"You really don't have to worry about Brose and me any more." My voice was sort of chokey.

"But couldn't you have gone on being friends?"

Older people are so naïve sometimes. I explained, "Brose didn't want to be friends after I got interested in Kim. And Kim didn't stay interested very long. At the moment," I said, striving for the light touch, "I seem to be fresh out of men."

"Is that what's the matter?" Mom asked, leaning toward me earnestly. "Because if it is, dear, there's nothing to worry about. Why, you've always had plenty of beaus. And you will again."

I patted her hand. I knew she meant well, that she wanted to help. She was really sweet. "Sure, I will," I agreed. "Who's worrying?"

But to myself I added starkly, "Will you get one in time for the Prom, though. That is the question . . ."

Chapter Twenty

GRADUATION AHEAD

IT WAS spring. Midge and her pal Judy jumped rope and played Wild Horses, racing and whinnying all over our yard. The weather was wonderful, warm sunshine and heavenly blue skies. The air was fresh and buds were bursting and the grass looked bright green and soft as velvet. I felt terrible.

Dick Allen's spring vacation from college provided a small oasis in my desert of datelessness. We went to the movies and out to dinner and on Saturday night he took me over to Hilltown to a night club. He was lots of fun, always, but he didn't say a word about having me up college again. So I had a pretty strong hunch he must be dating someone there. Of course, there was no reason why he shouldn't.

He noticed right away that I was no longer wearing Brose's ring. "Fight?" he inquired, looking from my bare hand up into my eyes.

I nodded.

"Not over me, I hope?" Dick looked troubled.

"No."

"Must have been that guy who was teaching you act-ing," he remembered.

"Let's just skip it," I said sort of huskily. "It's all an-cient history now."

So we didn't talk about it any more. Dick showed me a wonderful time while he was home. But a week has only seven days and when this one was over my life seemed even duller than before.

Barbie had Sox fix up a double date for us. I drew Itchy Stearns, who used to be Kay Lamb's steady and who has been lone-wolfing it since their break-up. Itchy and I have known each other since third grade and while we weren't actually allergic, the evening wasn't very exciting. But it was better than sitting home listening to the record player or reading a magazine.

"Did he ask you to the Prom?" Barbie inquired anx-iously the next day at school.

"No, he didn't."

Barbie's eyes snapped behind her harlequin glasses. "He might have, considering Sox had to loan him money for his share of the evening!"

I couldn't help giggling, Barbie looked so indignant. "Maybe he didn't have enough money for the Prom, either," I suggested. "Anyway, don't worry about me. I'll live, even if I don't get to go. Other girls have, you know."

Barbie sighed. I sighed, too, but I tried to keep it in-audible. Not to get invited to the Senior Prom was a thing I had never dreamed could happen to me. The Prom is the big social event of the year at high school, more im-portant even than the Heart Hop. It isn't held in the school gym, as the other dances are, but at Edgewood Country Club, with an imported orchestra and all the trimmings. The boys save up date money for months ahead and not to be invited to the Prom is enough to give any senior girl nightmares. Of course, there are always quite a few who aren't invited, because of one thing or another. Some of the senior men date younger girls and some of the senior girls don't have a steady boy they can count on. When I'd been wearing Brose's ring, I'd figured on our going to the Prom together. And when I'd had such a terrific crush on Kim, I'd supposed naturally that he'd ask me. Now I was experiencing the bitter hurt of being left out in the cold. But I was going to keep my chin up if it killed me.

Apparently my front had Barbie fooled. She said, "I don't see how you can be so calm about it. I'd be simply sunk!"

"Oh, well," I said drily, "it's just a dance."

But at home I couldn't help moping. I could feel my parents' sympathy wrapping me around like a warm cloak, although they were too tactful to say anything. And even Midge went out of her way to be a shade less poisonous than usual. A girl is really lucky to have a family like mine.

One day I came dragging in from school to find no one at home but my little sister. It was Mom's day at Woman's Club, I remembered. Midge was deep in a horse book, curled up in a chair in the living room.

"Where's Judy?" I asked, since they were always together.

"Sniffles," Midge said. "What you going to do, Tobey?"

"Might as well get my homework out of the way," I said. Leaving my evening clear for—what, I wondered? Maybe I'd call Barbie later and see if she wanted to go for a walk or anything.

I took my books upstairs to my room. A few minutes later I heard Midge turn on the radio, deafeningly loud as she always plays it, so I shut my door. I did my Math assignment first, since Math is always tough for me. Then I started in on English Lit.

"Tobey," Midge knocked on my door, as I had managed with considerable difficulty to train her to do. She opened it as I answered and stuck her head around the edge. Her eyes looked serious. "There's somebody downstairs to see you."

"Who?" I asked, getting up.

"Brose," Midge whispered.

I stared at her blankly. "Brose Gilman?"

Midge gave me a little push. "He didn't say what he wanted, just asked for you. I told him to wait in the library."

I took time to freshen my lipstick and give my hair a few quick passes with the brush. It was unbelievable, Brose downstairs, wanting to see me. What on earth for, I wondered, my heart beating rather fast. But it was silly to get this excited over Brose. We meant nothing to each other any more. But—why was he here? I was completely mystified.

Midge stood at the top of the stairs, watching me go down. Not until I reached the bottom did I hear her stealthy steps descending behind me. It would be just like the little squirt to listen to whatever Brose had to say. I went into the library and closed the door quietly behind me. That would show her!

Brose was sitting on the couch, idly turning the pages of a magazine. He shoved it aside and got to his feet as I came toward him. He looked just the same as always, big and dark-haired, his corduroy shirt unbuttoned at the throat. Nothing to get into a tizzy about as I seemed to be doing.

He said, his tone sort of questioning, "Hi, Tobey."

"Hello, Brose." I made a little motion for him to sit down again. Then I perched opposite him on the edge of a chair.

We looked at each other. Neither of us said anything. After a minute we both started to speak at once. "What did you—" I started to say. And Brose began, "What was it—"

Then we both stopped and waited. I could feel myself

flushing uncomfortably. It seemed so silly to feel ill at ease with Brose. Even though there was nothing between us any more, we were too well acquainted to get tied in knots this way.

I started in again with all the calm and dignity I could muster, "What did you want to see me about, Brose?"

He looked at me blankly. "That was what I was just going to ask you."

Now it was my turn to look blank. "But—Midge said you wanted to see me."

"Yeah, but not till you called me up and asked me to come over."

"*I* called you up?" I repeated incredulously.

"Well, sure," Brose frowned, "not more than fifteen minutes ago. Your radio was going so loud I could hardly hear you. And you hung up before I could ask what you wanted."

Light broke then blindingly. My dear little sister, sticking her dear little nose into things that didn't concern her! "I didn't call you," I corrected firmly. "It was Midge. She turned the radio up so you wouldn't recognize her voice. She—" a sudden, shattering thought struck me. I jumped to my feet and ran across the room to the door. It was locked, just as I had a hunch it would be. "Midge Heydon!" I exclaimed venomously. "Unlock this door this minute! You hear me?"

There was no sound other than Brose's footsteps behind me. He, too, tried the door.

"It *is* locked," he said in surprise.

I jiggled the knob furiously. "Midge, if you don't unlock this—"

My voice trailed off. She wouldn't unlock the door. I was simply wasting my breath ordering her to. I should know. This was the identical stunt I'd pulled on my sister Alicia the time she'd had such a terrific row with Adam Wentworth on the very eve of their wedding. I'd got Adam to the house by pretending on the phone that I was Alicia. Then I'd told her he was waiting in the library to see her. And when she had gone in, I'd locked the door.

140

The trick had worked perfectly. They'd made up. So now Midge had decided to try a repeat with Brose and me. But it wouldn't work this time. She'd see!

I turned to face Brose. "We may as well sit down and wait. Midge won't let us out till she's good and ready, or till Mom gets home. Of all the low tricks!"

We went back and resumed our seats stiffly. Or at least I felt stiff. Brose started grinning. "Now I remember where she got this idea."

"Let's not discuss it," I said aloofly.

"Why not?" Brose asked. "Seems to me this'll be as good a chance as we'll ever have to discuss a lot of stuff."

I opened my mouth to speak, but Brose said, "Wait a minute! Let me get some things off my chest first. Then it'll be your turn. I want to know why you've been avoiding me lately. Am I poison, or something? Just because that drip Fairbanks gave you the business, is that any reason to be so snooty with me?"

"I haven't been snooty," I denied.

"What else do you call it?" Brose demanded. "You just barely speak to me at school and hurry on like I got measles."

"I had no idea you noticed," I said. "You always seem so occupied with Mary Andrews."

"Now that's silly," Brose said. "I haven't been seeing any more of her than any other girl, only when she was helping me with my French."

I dragged my eyes away from his. "I'm sure I'm not interested."

"Well, I'm interested in you," Brose said bluntly. "Always have been, always will be, I guess."

My eyes swung back to his face in surprise. I asked huskily, "You mean—even after everything?"

"So you got tangled up with a phony," Brose said with a litle shrug. "Anybody can be mistaken in a person. I had to learn the hard way about Kentucky Jackson last summer. But you didn't hold it against me all the rest of my life."

It wasn't nearly as painful as I'd thought it would be, admitting, "You were right about Kim all the time."

"Forget it," Brose said. He reached out and laid his big hand over mine. I felt as though I were melting inside. "Don't waste your breath talking about him. It's us I'm interested in. Can't we be friends, like before?"

"Yes," I said, my eyes wide on his, "if you want to."

He asked the question then I'd been dreading to hear. "Will you wear my ring again?"

My throat hurt a little, my lips felt stiff, trying to form the words I wanted to say. I'd done a lot of thinking these past weeks. I'd had plenty of time for it. But I could back down, I needn't tell Brose what I'd decided. If I kept still, everything would be fine. I'd have the security a boy's class ring on your finger gives you, I'd never have to worry about a date. Brose would take me to the Prom.

But I couldn't just ignore my convictions. I had to be honest with Brose. He had a right to know how I really felt.

I said, "I don't want to wear your ring, Brose. I think maybe we've grown up too much for that." At his look of astonishment, I hurried on, "It isn't that I don't like you just as well as before. I do and I want ever so much for us to be friends again. But—well, when I wore your ring, I felt guilty every time I got a little interested in anyone else. It didn't seem fair to you. And it works both ways. You could change your mind about me. I want us both to feel free to go out with other people if we want to. We're young yet. So many things can happen. Can't we be friends without the ring, Brose?"

He sat there, looking deep into my eyes, his hand still clasping mine. At least, he wasn't mad. I'd done all right so far. Maybe a little more convincing would make him see things my way.

I reminded him, "Next year, you'll be away at college. Neither of us would want the other to feel guilty every time we had a date with anyone else. It wouldn't make sense."

"Yeah," Brose said thoughtfully, "but until I do go—"

I broke in, "I can't take your ring, Brose. Much as I'd like for us to make up, I won't wear it."

Brose said, "I want us to make up, too. Gee, all the fun of graduation, the Prom and all, would be spoiled if we weren't back together. It—just wouldn't seem right."

I nodded. I felt exactly the same way.

After a long moment, Brose said, "I suppose the ring really isn't important in itself. It's the way we feel about each other that counts."

"Oh, Brose—" that seemed to be all I could say. He was so wonderful, sitting there holding my hand tight and understanding all the things I was having such a hard time putting into words. I didn't feel as if I'd ever truly appreciated him until this minute.

He leaned toward me and I leaned toward him and our lips met. It was the most momentous kiss I had ever had in my whole life. Quite the most momentous!

Just as it ended, I heard the very faint unobtrusive sound of Midge unlocking the library door and sneaking away.

Little sisters are often a trial, but they do have their wonderful moments! I'd be the last person in the world to deny it.